# ALL I EVER WANTED

## RHAYNE

**All I Ever Wanted**



K & K Publishing Express
Moultrie, GA www.kkpublishingexpress.com

# Acknowledgment

I want to give thanks to Our Heavenly Father for blessing me with my creative talent, without him none of this would be possible.

I would also like to thank everyone who believed in me, supported me, and encouraged me along the way. I want you to know that I genuinely appreciate every one of you.

# Table Of Contents

# Part One

# In The Beginning

## McKenzie

Today started like any other day. I woke up to the smell of freshly brewed coffee and the aroma of breakfast lingering in the air. I knew Sharon was working her magic in the kitchen like she does every morning before I leave for work. I got out of bed, did my morning hygiene routine, and went downstairs. There were homemade biscuits, bacon, and eggs on the table.

"Mmm, this looks good?" I went over to Sharon and took the plates from her hand that she had just taken out of the cabinet. "Good morning, babe."

She kissed me on the mouth. "Good morning."

I sat down at the table and watched as she scurried around the kitchen. I thought about how lucky I was to have her in my life.

We met six years ago at James Emerson's birthday party. James is a good friend of mine, and I later found out Sharon and Amanda- James' wife, were best friends, so we were destined to meet sooner or later.

The night I met Sharon, she took my breath away. I still remember what she was wearing. She had on this sexy red spaghetti strap dress that clung to her body, showing off her plump breast and all of her curves, which by the way, were in all the right places. She was wearing silver stilettos and had a matching small silver purse to complete her attire. Her hair was in an up-do off her shoulders, and her make-up was flawless. She looked good, and all eyes were on her when she walked into the room. Amanda went over and hugged her. They talked a few minutes before Amanda gestured for me to come over. As I walked towards them, I thought about what I was going to say and prayed I didn't say anything stupid. I took a deep breath, trying to stay calm because my nerves were on edge. I wanted to know this woman at every level, and I didn't want to screw up my chance before it even began.

I'd been  focused on getting my architecture company up and running. I hadn't dated in two years, so I was very rusty when it came to approaching women. However, I have to say all the hard work paid off. I own one of Chicago's top architectural companies. Although business was great, I wanted a companion in my life.

As I stood in front of the woman who had stolen my heart at first sight, I didn't wait for an introduction. I cleared my throat, held out my hand, and said, "Hi, I'm McKenzie Taylor." She took my hand and a bolt of electricity shot through me. Then and there, I knew I would give anything to have her in my life. "Sharon Jenkins." She smiled, and my heart skipped a beat. Sharon didn't know it, but at that moment, she held the key to my heart.

"McKenzie, McKenzie!"

I snapped out of my trance. "Huh?"

"How many teaspoons of sugar do you want in your coffee?"

"Oh, I'll take two."

She smiled. "What's on your mind this morning?"

"You."

"Me."

"Yes, you."

"Hmmm, so what about me," he asked seductively.

"I was thinking about the first time we met. Do you have any idea how much I love you?"

"No, how much?" She walked over to me and wrapped her arms around my neck.

"To infinity."

She kissed me and sat back down. "Me too."

"So, what are your plans for today?"

"Well, Amanda and I are going shopping. She wants to buy a few more items for the baby nursery. The baby will be here any time now."

"Yeah, I know."

I didn't bother to hide the hint of sadness in my voice. I wanted a child, but Sharon wasn't interested in starting a family right now. She made that clear each time I brought up the subject. I often wondered would she ever come around.

I finished my breakfast, took an apple from the fruit bowl on the kitchen counter, and kissed Sharon on the cheek.

"I will be working late tonight," I said as I walked out of the kitchen.

"You've worked late every night this week. I was hoping we could go out to dinner and catch a movie tonight."

I stood in the kitchen doorway. "Babe, I have this huge project I'm working on, and I haven't completed  the blueprints. I promise I will make it up to you."

Sharon got up from the table and started washing the dishes. I watched her rake the food from her plate into the trash. She didn't say anything, but I knew she was angry.  I couldn't help it. I had to finish the blueprints. We were planning to start construction in three weeks. And with Byron Jefferson, CEO of Princeton Enterprises, continuously making adjustments, I wasn't sure if we would break ground as scheduled.

I walked back over to Sharon. Wrapping my arms around her waist, I kissed her on the neck. "I'm sorry, babe. This is a major contract. I have to make sure things get done and get done correctly. It's my name on the line. I'm the boss, remember?"

"I understand that, but I'm just asking for tonight. You shouldn't have any problems getting off early today, right, boss?" She asked with a hint of sarcasm.

"I can't."

"You can't or you won't?"

"Sharon, this is business. I promise once the job is complete, we are going to do something. Please be patient with me."

"Yeah, I hear you."

I kissed her on the cheek. "I'm gone I'll call you later."

When I entered the office, Sylvia looked up from her desk and smiled at me.

"Good morning, Mr. Taylor."

"Good morning, Sylvia. How are you today?"

"I'm doing well, and you?"

"I could be better. I'm going to have to figure out a way to get out of the dog house."

Sylvia had an inquiring mind, with that 'want to know' look on her face.

Sylvia is a fifty-six-year-old widow, with mahogany skin, short, salt, and pepper hair that accentuates her face. She still maintains the figure of a twenty-year-old, by going to the gym five days a week and eating a healthy diet. We have developed a mother and son relationship. She listens to me and gives me advice, motherly advice. She has been working for me since I opened my office seven years ago. She is God sent. I don't know what I would do without her.

"Have a seat," she said, with the nod of her head.

I sat in one of the burgundy leather chairs in front of her desk. "Sharon is mad with me for working late all this week," I sighed.

"Well, you have been working a lot and not just this week, but for a while now. You know what they say about all work and no play."

"God knows I have tried to get you to take off and spend some time with your wife. Now, I want you to listen to me, and you listen carefully. It's more to life than work. It's not good for a woman to feel lonely in her marriage. When she gets tired of being alone, she will begin searching for companionship somewhere else. That makes it very easy for another man to step in. Do you understand what I'm saying?"

"Ms. Sylvia, I hear what you're saying, and I'm trying. You know this is a big project. I have to get it done."

"Oh, I know you hear me, but you aren't listening. You can still get the project done and make time for your wife in the process. Don't get so caught up in work that you put her on the back burner."

"I am as soon as I complete this project. I just wish Sharon would be more understanding."

"Well, I tell you what. You better get your priorities straight. You shouldn't let anything come in between your marriage. If you need to hire an assistant to help mitigate the workload, do that. Now, I'm going to let you get to work, and I'm going to get back to working on this order."

I stood to go to my office. "I need you to send Sharon a dozen long stem red roses for me."

"Uh, huh, and what would you like written on the card?"

"Just have them put, I'm sorry."

"Okay, I'll get right on it."

"Thank you."

I walked into my office and sat at the desk. I started reminiscing about my conversation with Sylvia. I know she's right. It's time for me to make my wife a priority. I smiled. Sylvia Johnson always had a way of setting me straight and getting me on the right path, just like my mother used to do.

Both my parents were killed in a car accident three years after I started my architecture business. They were heading home from a medical convention when my father had a heart attack while driving and ran into a semi-truck. The police officer said they were both deceased when he arrived on the scene, and by the looks of the accident, neither one of them suffered.

Over time, Michael, Symone, and I got past their deaths and found the strength to move on with the love and support of each other. My sister, Symone, the youngest of us three, lives in Atlanta with her husband, Randy, and their two children. My brother, Michael, lives in Trenton, New Jersey, with his wife,

Vivian, and their three children. Michael is the oldest. Yes, I am the middle child and the only one without any children.

I am thirty-five years old with a successful business, a beautiful wife, and a lovely four bedroom home. All that's missing is little feet running around, but Sharon's not trying to hear it. Her argument is that I wouldn't have time to be a father because I am always working. I know that comes from anger, because I'm not spending time with her right now, but things are about to change. I know I would be a great father; if only she would get on board with starting a family. I looked down at the blueprints and thought about how I could make things right with her, and it came to me. I'm going to surprise her with a week's vacation in the Bahamas. I know she's going to love it.

## Sharon

Last night was beautiful. McKenzie and I made love, and we were so in sync with each other. It has been a long time since I felt so much passion. However, after we made love, he brought up the topic of children. I know he wants children, but I keep telling him not right now. I am thirty-two years old, and I'm not ready to be tied down with a child. There are still places I want to go, and things I want to see.

He provides a pleasant and comfortable living for us, and I enjoy the freedom to come and go when I'm ready. He is hardly home anyway, so I don't understand why he's so focused on wanting to start a family. A child would only complicate things for me.

I got up this morning and cooked him a big breakfast, thinking it would smoothen things out. I was also hoping he would take the evening off and spend it with me. But oh no, he has to finish the blueprints on this big project. Since this project started, I've been on the back burner. It seems he doesn't care about anything but his work and, of course, having a baby, which is not going to happen.

I have been very patient with him, but I'm getting tired of being alone. I've tried to occupy my time by going to the gym and hanging out with my girl, Mercedes.

Mercedes Wilkerson is twenty-eight and single with no children, so she has a lot of free time. When she's not working, we frequent Geri's bar to have some drinks and do a little dancing, which I love to do.

Most of the men there are real gentlemen. The ones that frequent there like Mercedes and I know that I'm married and they respect that. We are all there to have a good time; to unwind from the hustle and bustle of the day.

When the two of us are not at the bar, we go shopping, to the movies, or hang out at each others home. Sometimes, we include Amanda. The three of us have been friends for a long time, but since Amanda is pregnant, she doesn't get out as much as she used to.

Amanda and I are fortunate to have husbands who provide for us, so we don't have to work. The difference between us is she wanted children, and I don't. Some may call me selfish, but I don't care. This is my life, and I will live it the way I want.

Today, Amanda and I are going shopping for the baby. She and James have asked McKenzie and me to be godparents. Of course, we said yes. McKenzie was ecstatic, and to be honest, so was I. I know that may sound crazy, but remember, it's their baby, not ours. I can always give it back.

I called Amanda and told her I was on my way. When I pulled up in front of her Victorian-style home with a manicured lawn, she was already standing on the front porch waiting for me. Her stomach looked as if she had swallowed a basketball. She waved at me and began wobbling towards the car.

"Hey girl, what's up?" I smiled.

"Not a thing."

"Do you feel up to this adventure today? It looks like you are about to pop."

"I'm fine. I've been waiting on this day for a while, so I'm more than ready. Although I will admit I can't wait until this baby gets here, it's been hell on my back." she said with a small chuckle as she struggled to get in the car.

"I hear you. Where would you like to go first?"

"Let's go to Kiddie Styles. I want to look at what they have. There's a sale on their baby furniture, and I need a changing table."

"Okay, to Kiddie Styles, it is."

"So, tell me, when are you going to join the motherhood club?"

"Never!"

"Oh, come on, Sharon." Amanda teased. She knew where I stood about having children.

"Amanda, don't you start. You know I don't like talking about me having children."

"Yeah, I know, but I thought you may have had a change of mind by now since you did agree to be the Godmother of our child."

"Listen to me. I love you. You are like a sister to me. I love that baby you are carrying, and I plan to be the best Aunt/Godmother you could ever ask for. But I do not want a child of my own."

"Why?"

"Amanda, let's just change the subject.," I said as I turned into the parking lot of Kiddie Styles.

We went to three different stores before she finally settled on a cherry oak changing table with two drawers on the bottom that had little teddy bears carved in them from Baby's First Store. It was beautiful, and it matched the other baby furniture she already had.

Then we went to lunch at Charlie's, an Italian restaurant. Charlie's has been around for a very long time. The atmosphere is warm and inviting, and the staff is always friendly. It's one of my favorite places to eat. After being seated, we both ordered a salad, Italian chicken with pasta, garlic sticks, and sweet tea. We laughed and talked about our lives, the baby, fears, and dreams, etc.

"You know, Sharon, I really miss this."

"Me, too."

"After the baby, we are going to have to do this more often."

"Yes, we are." I smiled. "You ready to get out of here?"

"Yes, I'm full and ready to take a nap now."

We both laughed.

"I know what you mean."

I turned into Amanda's drive. James was sitting on the porch. He came to the car and helped Amanda up the steps. He is such a sweetheart. She's a lucky girl, I thought to myself, as James got the dresser out of the trunk of the car.

"Sharon, I appreciate you taking me around today."

"Girl, you know you are welcome anytime."

"Hey, I want you to look at the nursery if you have time."

"Oh, yes, I would love to see it."

The nursery theme was Winnie the Pooh. It was yellow, with a large tree painted in one corner of the room. The leaves fell from the tree to the ground as if the wind was blowing. There was a beehive sitting on one of the limbs with honey dripping from it and four bees swarming around the hive. Winnie the Pooh and Tigger were napping under the tree with their bellies protruding from overeating. There was green grass surrounding the tree, continuing around the room as if coming from out of the floor. There were clouds painted on both walls surrounding the tree. The wall on the left side of the room, which the crib rested against, had the baby's name spelled out with colorful alphabet pillows, "**BRIANNA**." The ceiling had little crystals in the paint that sparkled. When the lights were off, it looked like twinkling stars.

"Amanda, this is beautiful."

"Thank you. It's not finished yet, but we are close. We have a little more work to do on it."

"Well, so far, so good." We talked another thirty minutes about ideas for the nursery then I headed home.

Since McKenzie was working late tonight, I decided I would take a nap, then call Mercedes to see if she would like to go to Geri's for drinks.

When I got home, there was a white van with Justin Flowers Services written on the side of it, parked in the driveway. The driver, a handsome young man with beautiful mahogany skin and a gorgeous smile, began walking towards my car.

"Hello. I have a delivery for Sharon Taylor."

"I'm Sharon Taylor."

"Well, in that case, these are for you," he said, handing me the long red box he was holding.

"Thank you."

I gave him a five-dollar tip and sent him on his way. I opened the box, and there were a dozen long stem red roses inside. The card read: I'm sorry. I love you, McKenzie. They were beautiful, but they didn't make me feel better. You see, he is always buying me gifts or sending me flowers, as an attempt to make up for him not spending time with me. But I can't cuddle with roses. I laid the flowers on the table and called Mercedes. So much for my nap.

Mercedes picked up the phone after two rings.

"Hey girl, what are you doing?"

"Nothing much, what you been up to?"

"I've been trying to stay busy. McKenzie is still working on that project, so tonight is going to be another late night," I said disappointedly.

"Oh, well, that sucks."

"Tell me about it. Anyway, I was calling to see if you would like to go to Geri's tonight for some drinks. You know tonight is ladies'night, and that means a lot of fine men are going to be up in there."

"Sounds good to me, but I could care less about meeting any men. The ones I have been dating lately, either want you to take care of them or they're married; some even married with children."

"I know, girl, but maybe Mr. Right will be there tonight. You can't give up."

"Yeah, you know, some men are intimidated by a woman who has it together."

"That's true, but there are some men out there who want an independent woman and are not intimidated by her success."

"Well, I wish he would come my way."

"In time, he will," I tried to assure her. "Let's meet at Geri's at eight o'clock."

"Okay, that sounds great."

I hung up the phone and began looking for something to wear. I finally settled on a black, sleeveless jumpsuit and black heels.

It was six o'clock when I woke up to the ringing of the phone. I had dozed off to sleep. I fumbled for the phone on the nightstand.

"Hello," I said in a sleepy voice.

"Hi, babe, it's me. What are you doing?"

"What does it sound like I'm doing? I was taken a nap."

"I'm sorry to wake you, but I haven't heard from you all day.  I was wondering, did you receive the flowers I sent."

"Yes and they are beautiful, thank you. What time will you be home tonight?"

"Around twelve o'clock."

"Okay."

"Mercedes and I are going to Geri's to have some drinks. I will be home by the time you get here."

"Okay, have fun. Let me get back to

work. I'll see you when I get home. I love you."

"I love you, too."

When I walked into Geri's, right away I spotted Mercedes sitting at our favorite table in the corner, and the fact that she was standing up waving me over didn't hurt either.

"Hey girl, I see you started without me," I said, sitting down at the table. She was drinking her first cosmopolitan martini.

"Girl, yes, It's been a long day. I thought I would never get out of that office."

I signaled for the waiter. When she got to the table, I ordered an apple martini.

"So, girlfriend, what's up? You sounded like you needed to talk," Mercedes said, taking a sip of her drink.

"Girl, its McKenzie. He's working all the time and not spending any time with me. Sometimes, I feel like meeting someone else just to have a little fun, you know, a side thing."

"Sharon, you shouldn't talk like that. There are plenty of women out there who would love to be in your shoes. McKenzie is a good man. It's not like he's out there chasing women. The man is at work, providing you with all those luxuries you love so much. When he finishes this project, I'm quite sure he will make up for all the time lost."

"Yeah, that's what he said."

"Well, doesn't he keep his word?"

"Sometimes, but there are other times when he comes up with one excuse after another. Our sex life is almost non-existent. Hell, I had to work hard last night to get it. I pulled out all the stops, but once he got into it, it was good!" I said, giving her a high five.

"But keeping it real, for the most part, I have to have fun by myself; you know what I mean."

"Really? You're going to ask me that? Hell yeah, I know what you mean. I'm a single woman, remember? You know the only sex going on in my house is Mr. Tickles and me. I make sure I always have double batteries."

We both started laughing.

"Girl, you're crazy! I needed that laugh."

"Sharon, you have so many things to be thankful for. At least you have a man. I have been by myself for a year, and I tell you, I wish I had a man to take care of me and to cuddle up with at night. You, my dear friend, are whining about nothing. Stop acting like a spoiled brat and be more supportive of your man. It's going to all work out. Give it time."

"See, you are always taking up for him."

"Honey, it's not about taking up for him. I'm trying to keep you grounded. Don't do something stupid that will mess up your marriage. Girl, there is nothing out there. You see what I've been going through."

"I know, but it doesn't mean I have to like it. You know, last night, he brought up the subject of having a baby."

"Well, why don't you? You've been married for five years. I can understand him being ready to start a family."

"You would, wouldn't you?" I said, rolling my eyes at her. "I don't want any children. You and I have had this conversation several times.

"No, you keep saying you don't want any children, but you never say why."

"Why do you keep acting like having a baby is no big deal?" I asked, feeling frustrated about this whole baby thing.

"I guess because I come from a large family, and I want to have a family of my own someday."

"Well, good for you, but I don't ever want any."

Mercedes signaled for the waiter to come back to the table. We both ordered another round of drinks and Buffalo wings. When the waiter left, a tall, sexy, chocolate brother approached our table.

"Hi ladies, how are you tonight? May I have this dance," he asked, extending his hand to Mercedes.

"I don't dance with strangers," Mercedes said.

"Well, in that case, let me introduce myself. I'm Richard Madison, and you are?"

*What a delicious piece of chocolate*, I thought as I scanned his tall frame.

"Mercedes Wilkerson," she said, smiling from ear to ear. She took his hand and followed him to the dance floor. My girl has moves.

They were bumping and grinding on the dance floor. All they needed was a room. I could see the chemistry between them, and they looked good together.

The waiter returned with our food and drinks. I helped myself to the wings while I watched the show Mercedes and Richard put on. When they returned to the table, I made myself scarce and told Mercedes I would call her the next day.

## Mercedes

I was at work when Sharon called me and asked me if I wanted to go to Geri's tonight. It was around four o'clock, and I was exhausted. Fridays are always busy.

I work as a paralegal at James & Randall Law Firm. We have meetings with clients on Fridays. By the time I hear problem after problem, all I want to do is go home, pour me up a glass of wine and listen to some jazz.

I love Kenny G. That man knows how to make some beautiful music. Anyway, I opted to hang out with Sharon. She sounded as if she needed a friend, plus it's not like I was going to be doing anything tonight anyway. Maybe I will meet Mr. Right.

It's hard to find a good man these days. The men I have encountered are either married or want someone to take care of them, and that's not going to happen. I work hard for my money, and I'm not about to give it to some man. I feel brothers are intimidated by me because I have myself together. I own my home, I drive a Lexus, my finances are in order, and of course, I'm not a bad looking chic.

Some people say I favor J. Lo. And yes, I have the body, too. I know I may sound conceded, but I'm far from it. I'm just telling you the facts. I'm a very humble person. I appreciate the many blessings I have received. I wish I had someone to share it with, who is on my level or better; not any of these scrubs I've been running into lately.

I arrived at Geri's around 7:45 pm and got us a table. Of course, I was early, so I ordered a drink; pomegranate cosmopolitan; my favorite, by the way, while I waited on Sharon.

I saw this handsome brother walk in. He was dressed in an ivory shirt and a pair of brown slacks. He made eye contact with me as he walked past my table to the bar. He sat down and ordered a beer. He glanced my way as he took a swallow of beer from the bottle. Please, Lord, let him come to my table.

After waiting about ten minutes, I accepted the fact that he was not coming. I started scoping out the bar to see what other potential prospects were there when I noticed Sharon looking around the bar for me. I started waving my arm back and forth to get her attention.

Once she was seated, we started talking, and of course, she began complaining about her husband. I always try to make her see things are not as bad as they may seem. Sometimes, I feel Sharon is trying to find excuses to justify her wanting to have an affair. I know it's just a matter of time because she keeps talking about it. But she has a good man. She doesn't want to compromise. At least the man is working and not hanging out in the streets. I just had to flat out ask her, why did she get married, and she had the nerve to say, "so he can take care of me." I wanted to curse her out, but I held my tongue.

Here I am, looking for a good man and she has one, but doesn't appreciate him.

I felt like tonight was going to change for me because that fine man I was telling you about finally walked up to our table and asked me to dance. We had a great time. We laughed and talked all night. Sharon left early, which was fine by me because I was on cloud nine.  I found my Mr. Right. He was everything I wanted in a man or so I thought.

## Sharon

It was after ten o'clock when I arrived home. I was shocked when I pulled into the driveway and saw McKenzie's car. He had left a note on the back door for me that read **MEET ME IN THE BEDROOM**. I opened the door and could hear the sweet sound of jazz playing. I walked upstairs to the bedroom. When I opened the door, I was surprised. The room was illuminated with scented candles, and rose petals were on the bed. There was a bottle of wine chilling on ice and two long stem wine glasses on the reading table in the corner of the room. McKenzie walked out of the bathroom.

"Hey babe," he said.

"Hey."

We shared a long passionate kiss, then he led me to the bathroom where there was a hot bubble bath waiting for us. He began undressing me. Once I was completely naked, he held me close and started kissing me. He undressed, and we both got into the tub.

After our bath, he gave me a massage with heated coconut-scented massage oil. He began caressing my breasts. He suckled one and then the other, as I released soft moans. He planted kisses all over my body until he got to the bud of my flower. He caressed it with his tongue, sending heat piercing through my body until I reached the peak of my arousal. He stopped and gently entered me. We became one with each stroke taking us to a place of ecstasy until we climaxed.

The ringing of the telephone woke me up. "Ugh, who could this be," I groaned, as I turned over to look at the clock on the nightstand. It's nine-thirty in the morning for God sakes. I noticed McKenzie was not in bed. I answered the phone and told Mercedes I would call her later. I went downstairs in search of McKenzie, only to find a note attached to the refrigerator door.

**I didn't want to wake you; I will be at the office. I will call you later. I LOVE YOU.**

That damn Byron is becoming a pain in the butt. I've never met him, and I already don't like him. McKenzie will never finish those blueprints if he keeps making changes.

I poured myself a cup of coffee and called Mercedes back.

"Hey, girl!" Mercedes said cheerfully. "I'm sorry I woke you up. I just couldn't wait to tell you about my night."

She was a little too excited for me, considering my mood.

"Uh-huh," I responded with less enthusiasm.

"What's wrong with you?"

"I'll tell you after you tell me about your night."

"Well, in that case, girl! Richard is the perfect gentleman. He's like a dream come true. He's a pharmacist, single, no children, and he was very attentive to my needs all night long. Girl, I have never met a man who made me feel so special."

"Mercedes, don't you think it's too soon for you to make such an assessment? I mean, you just met the man last night."

"Well, who pissed on your cotton? I know I just met him, but I can feel it. I know he's the one."

"Okay, I'm not going to argue with you. I hope he is the one. All I want is for you to be happy."

"Thanks. We are going on a date Friday night."

"Where are you going?"

"We're going to dinner and a movie. We're keeping it simple. I might even invite Richard in for a nightcap, if you know what I mean." Mercedes giggled like a schoolgirl.

"You are too much. Just be careful," I chuckled.

"I will."

"Okay, enough about my night. What's going on with you?"

"Girl, Byron, McKenzie's client called last night wanting to make more changes. When McKenzie designed the mall and made the model, he was happy with the design. Now, he wants a waterfall in the middle of the mall surrounded by plants and exotic flowers."

"So how long will it take for McKenzie to incorporate the changes?"

"I don't know. He's meeting with Byron this morning to go over  the changes. I know he wanted to have everything finalized and start construction in three weeks, but now with this change, I just don't know."

"Maybe it won't be too much longer."

"I sure hope not," I said with little hope. "Changing the subject. Girl, when I got home

last night, McKenzie was here."

"He was."

"Yes, and let's just say, it was hot in our bedroom last night. If our walls could talk!"

"Girl, you are so crazy."

"Honey, that man knows how to rock my world. My body is still tingling, just thinking about it."

They both laughed.

"Sounds like you two worked some things out."

"Yeah, we did."

"I hear you. I'm happy to hear it. You know I only want the best for you two."

"I know it. That's why I love you, my sister."

"I love you, too."

## McKenzie

Last night was wonderful. After I called Sharon and she told me she would be leaving Geri's early because Mercedes had hit it off with some guy, I decided to surprise her and head on home so we could spend some time together. I wanted her to know that I heard her, and I am going to try to make an honest effort to be a better husband for her.

I stopped by the supermarket and picked up a bottle of wine, candles, and some rose petals. I managed to beat Sharon home, so I hurried and put the wine on ice to chill, then went upstairs to our bedroom and ran a hot bubble bath. I left a trail of rose petals from the door to the bedroom, on the bed, and in the bubble bath. I put a Jazz CD in the player.

When Sharon walked into the bedroom, the look on her face was priceless. I could tell she was surprised.

"McKenzie," she said with a big smile on her face.

"Shhh." I pulled her into my arms and kissed her, and she kissed me back with such hunger, her appetite matching mine. I pulled her even closer so she could feel my hardness. I wanted her, hell I needed her. "Tonight is all about you, babe," and it was.

Now here I am at my office, waiting on Byron to show up. He called me last night, to tell me he wanted to talk to me about adding a waterfall in the middle of the mall. This change is going to set us back another month, at the least. We scheduled this meeting for nine o'clock, and he is now thirty minutes late. I tell you, if it weren't for the fact that he is paying me a great deal of money to do this job, I would have sent him packing a long time ago. He has been a huge pain in my butt since we started, not to mention a pain in my marriage as well.

It was ten o'clock when Byron finally decided to show up.

"McKenzie, I'm sorry I'm late. I got stuck in traffic; bad accident."

"It's cool, but next time, give me a heads up."

I valued my time and didn't appreciate him not letting me know he was going to be late.

We looked at each other; no words needed to be exchanged. My message was clear, and he understood.

"Okay, so tell me about this waterfall," I said, breaking the silence.

After going over the design, he promised there would be no more changes, and I could move forward with the plans. Just as we were wrapping things up, Sharon knocked on the door.

"Hi, sweetheart," I said, as she entered the office.

"Hi. I didn't mean to bother you. I came by to take you to lunch."

"Oh, you're not bothering me at all, especially when you're talking food. We were just finishing up. Sharon, this is Byron Jefferson, CEO of Princeton Enterprise. Byron, this is my wife, Sharon." They shook hands. Byron said his goodbyes and left.

"No more work for me today. I am all yours."

"Well, in that case, let's get you fed because you are going to need your energy."

I put up the drafts, and Sharon and I left for lunch.

The following day, we decided to visit James and Amanda. When we pulled up in the drive, James hurried to the car with a look of panic on his face. I got out of the car to find out what was going on.

"James, man, what's wrong?"

"Amanda is in labor. I'm getting ready to take her to the hospital."

"Well, where is she?"

"She's in the house. She said she had to use the restroom before we leave."

"Okay, well, I'll drive. That way, you can sit in the back with her."

"Thanks, man. My nerves are bad anyway." James said, patting me on the back.

When we walked into the house, Amanda was walking towards the door, and Sharon was following behind her holding her bag.

"Alright, guys, let's go have a baby," Amanda said.

I must say she was very calm for a woman about to give birth to her first child. Amanda instructed Sharon to call Chicago Memorial Hospital and Dr. Morgan to let them know we were on the way.

Fifteen minutes later, we were pulling up to the emergency entrance. James got out of the car and went inside the hospital to get the nurse and a wheelchair. Just when they got to the car, Amanda had a contraction. It must have been a hard one because she bent over and let out a painful cry. The nurse helped her into the wheelchair and took her straight to the labor room to be examined.

Afterward, Sharon and I were allowed in the room. Amanda told us she had dilated four centimeters, and it would probably be a while before she had the baby, and we didn't have to wait around. However, since we were going to be the godparents, we wanted to stay there until the baby was born. Little did we know it would be ten hours later before Brianna Nicole Emerson made her entrance into the world. She was 7lbs 3ozs and so beautiful. She looked like a baby doll with her thick, black, curly locks and those pretty round eyes, with her little button nose.

I had fallen in love with this little angel.

She would be the second female ever to steal my heart.

**Sharon**

After I got off of the phone with Mercedes, I decided I would surprise McKenzie and take him out to lunch. When I arrived at his office, I let myself in with my key. I heard voices coming from the conference room. McKenzie and a young man were busy going over paperwork. When I knocked on the door, they both looked my way. I apologized for bothering them and invited McKenzie to lunch. I must say I was surprised when he accepted. They wrapped things up right away. He introduced me to Byron, and I must say that Byron is a good looking man. He has beautiful green eyes and a smile that could melt hearts. He left shortly after we were introduced. When he told McKenzie, there would be no more changes. That was music to my ears.

The weather was beautiful, so we agreed to have lunch in Central Park. We stopped by Tony's sandwich shop and picked up a couple of sandwiches, drinks, and chips before heading to the park. Once we arrived there, we sat under a large maple tree by the pond.

"I'm glad we chose to have lunch out here today. The flowers are so beautiful, and the air is refreshing," I said.

"I am, too, but most of all, I'm glad to be spending this time with you. I know I've been working a lot and haven't been there for you like I should. Please be patient with me. I promise things will get better."

I kissed him on the mouth. "I know they will. Let's just enjoy this moment."

We finished our lunch and walked through the park. It felt like old times, laughing and talking. I can't remember the last time we've done that. After leaving the park, we caught a midday movie, and Afterward, we went home and started where we left off the night before.

The next day, we went to see James and Amanda. When we pulled up, James was looking scared. McKenzie and I hurried out of the car. I went straight into the house. I overheard James telling McKenzie that Amanda was in labor.

When I entered the house, I found Amanda in the bathroom leaning over the sink.

"Amanda, are you okay?"

"Yeah, I'm having a contraction. It should be over soon. I tell you, these things are coming more frequent and each one stronger than the last."

"Can you walk?"

"Yes. Will you grab my bag out of our bedroom please. It's on the bed."

"Sure." I got the bag, and Amanda and I headed for the door.

When we got to the hospital, she was taken to the labor room. She was given a vaginal exam and an epidural.

By the time Amanda started pushing, my nerves had gotten the best of me. I couldn't stand to see her in all that pain. I understand what people mean when they say "try pushing something the size of a basketball out of something the size of a lemon." I thought I was going to pass out when I saw the baby's head crown. I don't think I would ever want to have a baby.

Finally, after all of the waiting, Amanda gave birth to a baby girl. She was so beautiful. As I held her in my arms, my eyes begin to fill with tears. I will always remember this day. Now I know you probably think I've had a change of heart. Don't get me wrong. I love my goddaughter. But, having a baby is something I don't want to do.

**Three Months Later**

I KNOW THIS IS NOT WHAT I THINK IT IS! I thought as I leaned over the toilet to vomit. I can't be pregnant. I know I took those birth control pills every day and on time. This cannot be happening to me.

After I cleaned myself up, I got the pack of birth control pills out of my drawer in the bathroom. There were only the seven non- active pills left. I never take those because I always remember when to start my new pack. I looked at the calendar. I start my new pack Sunday, but today is Friday, and I still haven't gotten my period. OKAY DON'T PANIC! I'M A PANIC!!!!! OH MY GOD! OH MY GOD! THIS CAN'T BE HAPPENING! IT CAN'T BE HAPPENING! I'm DREAMING! WAKE UP SHARON!

I sat on the toilet and began to cry. This is not a dream; it's a nightmare. I went into the bedroom and grabbed my phone off the bed and called Dr. Morgan's office.

"Dr. Morgan's office. How may I help you?" The receptionist asked. I knew it was Denise. I had been going to Dr. Morgan for years.

"Hi Denise, this is Sharon Taylor. I need to see Dr. Morgan today. I have an emergency."

"Okay, can you hold?"

"Yes, I can hold." Lord, please let her be able to see me today, I prayed. Denise interrupted my thoughts.

"Mrs. Taylor."

"Yes," I said with my fingers crossed.

"We can work you in today at two o'clock. Is that okay with you."

"Yes, that will be fine."

"Okay, we will see you then."

I said thank you and hung up the phone. Four hours later, I was sitting in Dr. Morgan's office. I was saying a silent prayer when the receptionist called my name. She escorted me to the examination room. Although it was a short time, it felt like forever, before Dr. Morgan entered the room.

"Hello, Sharon, how are you?" Dr. Morgan asked.

"I'm not so well," I said.

"Well, explain to me what's going on."
"First of all, I am vomiting, eating more than usual, I've gained five pounds and my period is late."

Dr. Morgan raised her eyebrow. "How late are you?"

"Well, I'll start my new pack of birth control pills on Sunday, but as of today, I still haven't seen my period."

"Hmmm, do you think you may be pregnant?"

"I don't know. That's why I'm here," I snapped.

"Let's just see what's going on. For starters, pee in this cup, and we will run a pregnancy test. If it's negative, then we will explore other options. On the other hand, if it's positive, then you and McKenzie will have some celebrating to do," she smiled.

If looks could kill, she would've been dead, because I gave her the meanest, ugliest look I could give. You know the kind of look that says, 'Don't try me; I will hurt you.' I think she got the point due to the way she hurried out of the room.

The nurse came back and collected my urine sample. Fifteen minutes later, Dr. Morgan was sitting in front of me, telling me the test was positive and that the antibiotics I took last month to clear up a kidney infection must have weakened my birth control. I don't know what else she said, because everything went still. I just sat there with tears running down my face. I cleared my throat.

"Dr. Morgan, I don't want this baby."

A surprised look covered her face.

"Mrs. Taylor, I think you should go home, get some rest and discuss this with your husband."

I gave her a cold stare and repeated myself.

"I don't want this baby."

"I hear what you are saying, but before you make any decision, sit down and talk it over with your husband."

I nodded in agreement. There was no need to continue this conversation because she wasn't listening to me.

When I got home, I lay across the bed and cried myself to sleep. It was six o'clock when I woke up. McKenzie can never find out about this baby. I began looking in the phone book for the phone number to the Women's Choice Clinic. I found the number and called. I got a recording. Office hours are Monday through Friday from 8 am to 5 pm. I hung up the phone. Well, I'll just have to wait until Monday. This is going to be a long weekend.

## Mercedes

Richard is an incredible lover. These past three months have been very blissful. He is everything I ever wanted in a man. He is caring, considerate, passionate, and romantic. Most of all, he has the main three characteristics that are important to me; career, single, and no children. Don't get me wrong. I want children, but I don't want an already made family. I don't have time for the baby mama drama. I love my life the way it is, DRAMA FREE!

This past weekend, we went to visit my family in Springfield, IL. Richard fit right in, and that means a lot in itself. My family is big. My parents, Gerald and Diane Wilkerson, had eight children. Of course, I am the baby. I have five brothers and two sisters. Also, there is my Nana, Irene, who lives with my parents. Dad, Mom, and Nana loved Richard. Even my brother's Kevin and Derrick got along well with him, which says a lot since they have never liked any of the guys I dated in the past. He didn't get to meet any of my other siblings because they couldn't make it, but we had a great time. I enjoyed being home with my family; I've missed them so much.

When we returned to Chicago, we discussed the idea of him moving in with me. To tell you the truth, I was a little nervous about this arrangement at first, but now, I' m glad he moved in. It has been great. The only problem I have is he works four nights a week at this night club downtown called **GEMINI**. He doesn't want me at the club because he says the crowd is a rough group of people, but I don't buy it. I stopped complaining about it and just dropped the subject for a while anyway. What I don't understand is that Richard is making good money, so why is he working a part-time job? When I ask him, he says, and I quote, "he's helping out a friend because his bartender quit." But, when I ask him how long it's going to be before his friend finds a replacement, he says he doesn't know, there's no hurry. Oh, and another thing. This friend doesn't have a name, but one thing I know for sure, secrets have a way of coming out, and my momma didn't raise a fool.

## Richard

Club Gemini is really jumping tonight, Usually, it's not this busy on Mondays, but that's okay with me, it just means more money.

"What's up, Jimmy?" I said to my friend when I approached the bar.

"Nothing much, man, just holding it down. Where have you been?" He gave me a one-shoulder hug and a pat on the back.

"Aww man, I've got me a girl. She's fine as hell, too."

"Well, that explains why we haven't seen you in a couple of weeks. We thought something had happened to you. D and his boys have been out looking for you."

"Man, if you saw her, you would know why I've been MIA. Where is D at anyway?"

"He's in the back."

When I entered D' s office, he looked up from the paper he had spread over his desk.

"What's up?" I said.

"What's up is where the hell have you been these past two weeks? I have been looking all over this city for you. I was afraid you were somewhere dead, and you come in here like everything is happy go lucky," he snapped.

D stood up and walked around his desk, standing in front of me with his arms across his chest.

"What, cat got your tongue? I asked you a question."

D was angry, and it showed all over his face.

I let out a nervous laugh. "Um, I met this girl, and I was hanging out with her."

"So, you couldn't call me to let me know you were okay?" Without giving me time to answer, he continued. "You know Richard, if you weren't my little brother, I would whip your ass." He grabbed me and gave me a hug. "I'm just happy you are alive and not somewhere lying in an alley dead."

"I'm sorry, Bro, didn't mean to worry you like that."

"So, does this girl have a name?"

"Yes, Mercedes, and big bro, if you were trying to find me around these parts, then you were looking in the wrong place. She lives on the other side of town, in one of those nice suburbs."

"Oh, so, what you got you a rich chick now?"

"Nah, but she's an educated woman, very classy, not like some of those hood rats I've dated in the past. You know what I mean."

"Well, does she know what you do?"

"Hell no! And she never will."

## Sharon

Monday couldn't get here fast enough. I called the clinic , and she told me I could come in at eleven o'clock because they had a cancellation.

When I arrived, I signed in at the receptionist's desk. Now here, I am sitting in the lobby room waiting for someone to call me back so I can see the doctor. I am so nervous. My heart feels like it's going to jump out of my chest. I wish they would hurry up. I am ready to get this done and over with.

"Monique Smith." I stood and followed the nurse behind the open door leading to the back of the office. I didn't tell the receptionist my real name because I wanted to keep my identity hidden. Although she said everything was confidential, I couldn't take that chance.

"Monique, I'm going to need a urine sample," she said, handing me a small cup.

I took the cup and went into the restroom. After giving her the urine sample, she led me to a room where there were other women watching a video on abortions. I became sick looking at it, so I closed my eyes, I couldn't bear looking at what I was about to do to my unborn child. Shortly after the video ended, like clockwork, the nurse entered the room. She called my name and took me to an examination room. She began asking me a lot of questions.

"Monique, why do you want to have an abortion?"

"Because I am a single woman, and I cannot support this baby financially."

"Have you thought about giving the baby up for adoption?"

"No, that is not an option. I don't want to carry this baby for nine months just to give it to someone else. I don't want to be pregnant, period."

"Where is the father of the child, and is he aware of your decision to have an abortion?"

"I don't know who the father is. I had multiple partners," I responded.

When she finished her list of questions, she gave me a gown and told me the doctor would be in shortly. As I sat waiting for the doctor, I thought about McKenzie. I knew he would want this baby, but in my heart, I know I'm not ready to be a mother. There was a light tap on the door.

"Hi, I'm Dr. Freil, how are you doing today?"

"Nervous."

She placed a hand on my shoulder. "Everything will be fine." She assured me. "So, the nurse tells me you want to go ahead with the abortion."

"Yes."

"Are you sure about this? Once we start, there is no stopping."

"Yes, I'm sure. Will I be in a lot of pain?"

"You will have some pain and cramping, but I will give you something for them both."

"Okay," I said, happy to know I will have something to help with the pain.

"We are going to start an I.V. and give you something to help you relax. When you wake up, it will be all over. "Do you have someone with you to drive you home?"

"No. I will need a taxi."

"Okay, when you are out of recovery, I will have the receptionist call one for you."

"Thank you. Dr. Freil, will this take long?"

"Not at all, your just six weeks, so the procedure should be fast, provided there aren't any complications."

I shook my head and lay back on the table. I closed my eyes and said a prayer. I asked God to please let everything go smoothly and to forgive me for what I am about to do.

The nurse came into the room with a syringe full of clear liquid on a tray.

"Hi, my name is Samantha, and I will be assisting Dr. Freil with your procedure today."

She gave a warm smile, which made me feel comfortable like she wasn't judging me for having this abortion. She quickly put in my I.V. and injected the liquid from the syringe in it. She then told me to count backward from one hundred out loud. 100, 99, 98…

"Monique, Monique," I heard someone calling as I was being shaken. When I opened my eyes, Samantha was beside me.

"How do you feel?"

"I'm fine, a little sore."

"That's normal."

"Did everything go, okay?"

"Everything went well. I will let the doctor know you are awake."

"May I have a glass of water?"

"Sure, I'll be right back."

"Thank you."

Shortly after she left, Dr. Freil entered the room.

"Well, Monique, the procedure went well. You should have a speedy recovery. You need to get plenty of bed rest for the next couple of days. No heavy lifting, no mopping, sweeping, or vacuuming for the next two weeks. Here are your instructions and your medication for the pain. If you have any problems, call me, okay?"

"Okay."

"Do you have any questions for me?"

"No. Thanks for everything."

"Well, if you get home and think of something, feel free to call us back. The nurses are very informative about the procedures and the aftercare."

"Okay."

Samantha came in with my clothing and two small white cups.

"Here you go," she said, handing me two pills in one of the cups and water in the other one.

"Take these; it will help with the soreness and the pain. We have called a taxi, and it should be here shortly."

"Thanks," I said just before swallowing the pills.

By the time I got dressed, and released from the clinic, my taxi was outside waiting for me.

When I arrived home, I took a shower and got into bed. I made sure I hid all evidence of me having an abortion. The hard part was over. Now I have to make sure I don't let McKenzie know I'm in pain.

## McKenzie

"Mr. Taylor, your reservations have been made. You can pick up your airline tickets at the airport. Your flight departs tomorrow at 8:30 am."

"Thanks, Sylvia."

"You're welcome. You two have fun."

"Oh, I plan on it," I said, preparing to leave for the day.

When I arrived home, I found Sharon in bed. It was so unlike her to be in bed in the middle of the afternoon.

"Babe, are you okay?" I asked.

"I don't feel so good. I got my period today, and the cramps are just so bad."

"Can I get you anything?"

"No, I have already taken something for the pain."

"Okay, well, I have some good news that just might make you feel better," I said, excited about the surprise trip.

"What is it?"

"I made reservations for us to fly to the Bahamas. Our flight leaves in the morning."

"Oh no, McKenzie. You are going to have to cancel those plans. I don't feel like vacationing anywhere right now," she groaned.

"I appreciate the thought, but now is not a good time. I'm just too sick," she said, touching me on my arm..

"Sharon, it's only your period, you should be okay. Just take some medicine for your cramps."

"You are not going to stand there and tell me I will be okay. This is my body; I don't feel good, and I am not going to the Bahamas."

"Really, you are going to refuse to go on a trip because of your period? Where the hell they do that at?"

"McKenzie, I don't want to go! Now leave me alone!".

I could feel my blood getting heated. I was beginning to get pissed. This woman has been on my case for a long time about us spending time together. Now, I finally make plans to spend time with her, and she tells me she doesn't want to go anywhere.

"Okay, Sharon. I'll cancel the plans."

She didn't respond. She laid her head on the pillow and told me to close the door.

I went downstairs and poured me a double shot of Hennessy. I sat down at the table. First, I called the airline and canceled the flight. Then, I called and canceled the reservation at the Atlantis. When I finished my drink, I got in my car and headed to Geri's.

When I walked in, I spotted Mercedes at the bar.

"Hey, I'm surprised to see you here?" I said, trying to disguise the anger in my voice.

"I have a lot on my mind," she said.

"I understand that. Me too," I said, signaling for the bartender to come my way. I ordered a double shot of Hennessy.

"You want to talk about it?" She asked.

"I guess it would be nice to get a woman's perspective."

"Well, in that case, come into my office." She pointed at one of the tables.

We both laughed and sat down with our drinks.

"Mercedes, I know you are my wife's best friend, but I trust what we talk about you will keep between us."

"Of course, I will."

I think she could sense my hesitation.

"You have my word."

"I don't know where to begin. I guess I can start with this latest fiasco."

"Which is?" She inquired.

"I wanted to surprise Sharon, so I purchased two flights to the Bahamas. Our flight was leaving at 8:30 am, but when I got home from work this afternoon to tell Sharon about the trip, I found her in bed."

"Is she sick?"

"No, she said she got her period today and wasn't feeling well. When I told her about the trip, she told me to cancel it."

"Are you serious?" Mercedes interrupted.

"Yes, so I canceled the flight and reservation just before coming here."

"Why not just reschedule it?"

"I don't know. I just said the hell with it."

She nodded. "I can understand that," she commented.

"Mercedes, I went out of my way to make this happen, and she really disappointed me. To be honest, I'm hurt. I always try to do what I can to make her happy, but nothing seems good enough. You know, I'm about done trying."

"I believe she'll come around."

"Yeah, maybe. Anyway, I have a new client coming to see me next week. Hopefully, that will come through, and I will start working on it by September, if not sooner. We're already at the end of July, and I don't know when I'm going to be able to take off again."

"Is the mall going to be ready by September?"

"No, but I will be able to go back and forth between both projects.

"Well, what is this second job?"

"It's a shopping plaza with eight stores. It's small, but it will be around summer before both jobs are completed."

"I see." She said, taking a sip of her drink.

"Mercedes, let me ask you something."

"Okay, shoot."

"Is Sharon happy?" Mercedes took a swallow of her drink before answering. I studied her face carefully.

"McKenzie, what do you think?"

"I don't know, why are you not answering my question?"

"Because I don't want to answer that."

"Why not?"

"You know Sharon is my girl, and I don't want to get involved."

"Okay, I can accept that," I said, shaking my head in agreement.

"Well answer this. Do you think I am a bad guy?"

"No, from what Sharon tells me about you, I think any woman would be lucky to have you as a husband, and I tell her that all the time." She said with a smile.

"So, your friend doesn't think so, huh?"

"I'm not saying that. I'm just trying to say you are a good man. I would love to have someone like you in my life." And I would love to have a woman like you, I thought to myself.

I was shocked by this revelation. I have always admired how hardworking Mercedes is. She's a go-getter. Although she loves nice things, non-material-istic, she's very humble. I wish Sharon was like that. I looked away, hoping she didn't notice the desire in my eyes. She broke the silence.

"McKenzie, it will get better." She sounded so positive.

"I sure hope so," I mumbled. "Okay, enough about Sharon and me. What's going on with you?"

Mercedes let out a long sigh.

"Well, I don't know if Sharon mentioned to you about my boyfriend, Richard."

"Yes, she did." A feeling of sadness came over me. What the hell, this is Sharon's friend, stupid!

"When we first started dating, everything was great. Now, I can't pinpoint what is going on with him. He has taken a second job as a bartender down at this club call Gemini's. He works four nights out of the week and gets in at the wee hours of the morning. I have asked several times, could I go with him to the club and he not only tells me no but gets very upset with me. So, what's your opinion on that?"

"You mention this is his second job. What's his first job?"

"Oh, he's a pharmacist."

"What pharmacy does he work at?" I asked, more out of curiosity than anything.

"He works at Krystal pharmacy on 152nd street."

"Do you trust him?"

"Of course I do, but lately, I've been feeling a little suspicious."

"Why?"

"Because of all the late nights."

"Well, clubs stay open late, and he is the bartender. It's not like he can just up and leave before the club closes."

"I know, and I keep telling myself nothing is going on, but my intuition is telling me that something is not right, and you know what they say about intuition."

"ALWAYS FOLLOW YOUR GUT!" We both said simultaneously.

"So, why don't you go check it out?"

"Because I don't want him to think I don't trust him, and he said the club was on the rough side of town."

"If it was so rough, why would a pharmacist be working part-time in a place like that?"

"He said his friend owns this club, and he is helping him out."

"Oh, well, maybe everything is on the up & up. There's no harm in helping out a friend."

"That's what I keep telling myself."

We talked another half hour, finished our drinks, and said our goodbyes.

It was 9:30 pm when I arrived home. Sharon was sitting up in bed watching television.

"Hey, where have you been?"

"I went to Geri's. Why?" I said with a hint of anger in my voice. I wanted her to know I was still pissed off about having to cancel the trip.

"I just asked. When I woke up you were not here, so I was wondering where you went."

"Well, it didn't appear that you wanted me around anyway. After all, you told me to leave you alone."

"I told you I didn't feel good."

"Yeah, I know. Actually, I don't know. Out of the five years we've been married, your periods have never had you acting this way." I said, now getting heated again.

Sharon didn't respond. She lay back down and turned her back to me, and with that gesture, I turned and walked out of the bedroom.

**Mercedes**

"Hey babe, you miss me?" Richard's voice was deep and sexy.

"You know, I do."

"What are you wearing?"

"A black teddy."

"Are you in bed?"

"Yes."

"Put the phone on speaker." I did as he asked.

"Slip your hand in your panties."

I loved it when we have phone sex.

"Okay."

"Now, massage your bud, and picture me licking you."

"Hmmm," I moaned.

"I like the way you taste. Mmm, so sweet. Put your finger inside you and slide it in and out."

"Mmm."

"Take your other hand and play with your nipples, pinching them lightly while I'm sucking on your bud."

"Ooh, babe."

"Are you wet?"

"Now, I'm sliding my big juicy wood inside of you, can you feel it, babe?"

"Mmm, yes." I moaned.

"Ooh, babe, you're so wet."

"Yes, you got me so hot."

" Girl, you feel so good."

" Ooh Richard, I'm almost there."

"Cum for me, babe."

"Ooh, Richard, I'm cumin!" I yelled as I climaxed.

"Ooh babe, I'm cumin too." He moaned loudly.

"Richard."

"Yes, babe."

"I wish you were here."

"I know. I'll be home soon."

"Okay," I said, before ending the call.

I found myself thinking of McKenzie and the conversation we shared tonight. I wondered how things would be if I had a man like him. One who is thoughtful, caring, and would do anything to make his woman happy. Too bad, we are both with others who are selfish and only think of themselves.

It was three o'clock when Richard got home.

"Hey babe." he bent down to kiss me, and the smell of alcohol and stale cigarette smoke reeked from his clothing.

I turned my head. "Ugh! Go shower!"

"Oh, so it's like that?"

"Yes, it's like that. You stink!"

Richard didn't say anything; he grabbed his pajama bottoms and went to take his shower. When he got into bed, as soon as his head hit the pillow, he fell asleep.

This has got to stop. I don't know who he thinks he is, but things are about to change up in here. No more being the understanding girlfriend. He's going to get his act together or get out of my house. If I wanted to be alone, then I wouldn't have given him a chance.

I turned over, fluffed my pillow, and drifted off to sleep.

**Sharon**

"Hi Beautiful, you sure are looking good tonight."

I turned around to look at who the sexy voice behind me belonged to, and to my surprise, it was Byron Jefferson looking as good as ever.

"Well, hi, yourself. What brings you out tonight?" I asked

"Just need a little downtime."

"I hear you, same here."

"Care to join me at my table?" He turned and pointed to his table.

"Of course, I could use the company."

After we were seated and had ordered our drinks, Byron led the conversation.

"So, how is McKenzie?"

"He' s fine, but I don't want to discuss McKenzie tonight."

Byron raised his eyebrow. I could see the curiosity all over his face.

"It's a long story and one I don't care to talk about," I said.

"Okay, then no talking about McKenzie."

"Thank you," I smiled.

"You have a beautiful smile."

"Thank you. So, Mr. Byron, tell me a little about you."

"Oh, is this an interview?" He chuckled.

"No, it is not, I just want to get to know you," We both laughed.

"Well, I am the CEO of Princeton Enterprises, but you already know that."

"Yes, I do."

He smiled and continued.

"I am thirty-eight and single. I have a fifteen-year-old daughter that lives with her mom in San Diego. I live alone, and yes, I have a friend that I kick it with from time to time, but nothing serious. Now, what about you? What's your story?" He asked, taking a sip of his drink.

"Well, I am thirty-two, of course, you know I am married, but we have no children, and right now, things are not so good between us, which is why I am here in the first place."

"Do you want to talk about it?"

"No. I just want to have a nice conversation, do a little dancing, and forget about everything else."

"I can help you with that." He said as he took my hand and led me to the dance floor.

I had a great time with Byron, maybe too great of a time.

"I have to go," I said, standing to leave.

Before he could respond, I was heading for the door.

"Hold on," he yelled over the music as he moved towards me.

I stopped and turned around.

"I'll walk you to your car."

When we were outside, I hit the unlock button on my keypad to unlock my car.

"I would like to see you again," he said.

I was about to refuse his invitation when he covered my mouth with his. I parted my lips and our tongues locked together in a sensual dance, causing a tingling sensation between my thighs. I pulled away and took a deep breath.

How could I turn down this fine specimen of a man? I thought as I looked in his sexy brown eyes. Before I knew it, I had agreed to meet with him again. I took his business card and promised to call.

It was almost two o'clock when I arrived home, and McKenzie was sound asleep. Thank God for small miracles.

I quickly got a shower and eased into bed. I found it hard to sleep that night because I couldn't get my mind off Byron, his smell, his touch, the feel of his lips. The thought of it all had my brain working overtime.

The next morning, McKenzie and I made love. Afterward, he asked me where I was last night. I told him that I was at Geri's with Mercedes, and we were having such a great time that time just flew by. He didn't respond to that; he just got up and went to take a shower. I was glad because, if he would have kept questioning me, I knew he would have seen the lie all over my face.

After we both showered and got dressed, we decided to visit James and Amanda. It had been a couple of weeks since we've last seen them. After McKenzie spoke with James, it was agreed we would see them around 4:30 pm that afternoon.

When we arrived at their home, James was outside grilling steaks. I hugged him and continued in the house where Amanda was in the kitchen, preparing a green salad. Little Brianna was in her baby carrier, watching her mother's every move.

"Hey!" I said.

"Hi." We exchanged hugs. "Can I help you with anything?"

"No, this is all I have left to do," she said, putting the finish touches on the salad.

So, we talked, and I played with Brianna.

We had a great time at the Emersons. At least up until they told us they were moving to Atlanta in November. James had been offered a partnership at Edmond & Reese Law Firm. He's an excellent lawyer, so I'm not surprised that he made partner.

I am very happy for him but hate they have to move. McKenzie was sad too because he would no longer be able to hang out with his friend and wouldn't be able to see little Brianna. I, on the other hand, knew that the pressure for us to have children would follow after they moved, and I was not looking forward to that. In a way, Brianna had brought peace and balance in the Taylor's home.

Around nine o'clock, we said our goodbyes and headed home. The ride was tranquil. I knew McKenzie was having a hard time with this news, but in due time, he will get over it.

As for me, I was thinking about Byron. It had been three days since I last saw him. So, I decided to give him a call later on that night. We made plans to have lunch at Lagoon's Steakhouse. When I arrived at the restaurant, he was waiting for me at the entrance. He looked so good in his chocolate suit. He wore a cream shirt and a chocolate and cream tie with specks of gold in it. Mmm, I could eat him up.

As soon as I approached him, he pulled me to him and kissed me on the cheek. I wanted more, but I knew this was neither the time nor place for that. After all, I am a married woman.

We walked inside and were seated right away. The waitress came to our table, and we placed our orders. Since our conversation at Geri's, there was one thing that kept crossing my mind. I wanted to know who his companion was. So after the waitress walked away, I immediately asked him.

"Byron, the other night, you mentioned you have a companion."

He took a sip of his tea. "Yes, I do."

"Does this companion have a name?"

"Yes, her name is Renae. Why do you ask?"

"I don't know; it's just that you didn't mention her name the last time we were together, and I was curious."

There was a long pause.

"Sharon, I like you, and I want to get to know you better. I was upfront about my relationship with Renae because I didn't want any problems later. Are you going to be able to handle my relationship with her?"

"I don't know."

"Well, I want you to think about it, no pressure."

By the time the waiter came back with our food, our conversation was almost non-existent because my mind was miles away. I kept noticing Byron glancing over at me from time to time.

After lunch, he walked me to my car, and again, the scene from the other night repeated itself. He pulled me to him and kissed me. This time, the kiss was much more passionate than the other night; it woke up a hunger in me. I wanted him, and I knew he wanted me, too.

**McKenzie**

"Mr. Taylor, Mr. Lexington, is here."

Sylvia announced over the intercom. "Send him in."

McKenzie walked from behind his desk and held his hand out to greet Robert Lexington when he entered his office.

Robert is a junior partner of Kershaw's Realtors Inc., Kershaw specializes in building shopping plazas.

"Mr. Lexington, how are you?"

"I'm doing great, and you?"

"I'm doing great myself."

"That's good to hear. Mr. Taylor, I'm going to get right to the point. We have heard only great things about your company."

"I'm glad to hear that."

"Indeed, Indeed." Mr. Lexington nodded.

"Byron Jefferson speaks very highly of you. He said you designed and oversaw the construction of the Princeton Mall. I had a chance to see it this morning. I must say you have done a marvelous job."

"Thank you, sir," I smiled.

"You're welcome. Mr. Taylor, I have a business proposition for you."

"I'm listening."

"Our company wants to build six new shopping plazas in New York. We want you to design and oversee the project until it is finished.

"We are willing to compensate you quite well for your expertise. What do you say?"

"That sounds great, but if you don't mind, before I make a decision, I would like to look at the locations and see what all would have to be done."

"Okay, when do you think you will be able to come to New York?"

"I have to tie up some loose ends here and could probably be in New York by Monday."

"That sounds good to me. We will see you on Monday. We can go over everything then."

We shook hands. "See you Monday."

When I arrived home, Sharon was lying on the couch.

"Hey, babe."

"Hey, how was work today?"

"It was great. I got a new business proposal from Kershaw's Realtors."

"That's great!"

"Well, there's some good and bad news."

"Oh, really." She said, sitting up.

"Yes."

I took a deep breath preparing myself for the argument I was sure going to happen once I told her I would be working in New York.

"Okay, tell me what it is."

"You want the good news first or the bad news?"

"Tell me the good news first."

"Alright, the good news is they want me to oversee six shopping plazas," I said, full of excitement.

"What? That is wonderful!" She was just as excited as I was.

"Hold on, the bad news, remember."

"What's the bad news?" She sighed.

"The project is in New York."

With a hint of sadness in her voice, she asked.

"So, when do they want you to start?"

"I have to be in New York Monday. It will only be for three days, just long enough for me to visit the sites and handle the legal stuff. Should I accept the offer? Leo is going to fly out on Tuesday to look over the contract, so everything should be finalized by Wednesday afternoon. I should be home that evening."

I sat back and waited for the protest. There was none. I was surprised, especially since the job would be taking me away from home. However, on the other hand, she knows my profession sometimes takes me out of town. Maybe she's accepting things for what they are.

## Richard

Wednesday nights at Gemini's are always jumping.

The crowd was going crazy as Renae twirled around the pole. Men of all ages were waving their money back and forth trying to get Renae's attention.

She is one of the hottest dancers in Gemini's and one of the highest-paid. She has beautiful dark skin and is not bad looking on the eyes. Too bad these clowns think they could have a chance with her. They are constantly tipping her big and buying her all kinds of gifts in hopes that they would be the lucky ones. But she only has the hots and heart for one man, and that is Byron, her one and only true love.

I stood at the bar and watched the men go wild as each of the dancers did their routine. Since there weren't many people sitting at the bar, I decided to call Mercedes.

Sorry, we're not home, leave a message after the beep.

I looked at my watch. It was twelve o'clock. I know she should be home by now. She has to work tomorrow. I told Jerry I was gone for the night. When I got home, Mercedes' car was in the drive. I felt the hood of the car; it was cold. When I entered the house, I saw a light coming from the bedroom. I opened the door, and Mercedes looked up at me.

"Why didn't you answer the phone?"

"I didn't want to," she said with attitude.

"You had me worried."

"Well, if you were that concerned, you would have been here instead of at that damn club."

"Mercedes, you know I'm working. Why are you tripping?" I walked over to the bed and sat beside her. "The rest of the week is yours, I promise. I will not work at the club." I tried to kiss her, but she turned her head. "Babe, I'm trying. What else do you want me to do?"

"You know what, Richard. We have discussed this over and over again. I' m not going there with you tonight. All I' m going to say is, you need to start making more time for me and spending less of it at the club." Like that, she was finished with the conversation.

The following morning, I called D and told him I wouldn't be in the rest of the week but would be back Monday. He understood and told me to handle my business.

I prepared breakfast for Mercedes. When I was done, I woke her up with light kisses around her face and on her lips. She looked surprised at the beautiful breakfast I had laid out for her. There were pancakes, sausage, hash browns, fresh fruit, and orange juice.

"Thank you, babe. This is so sweet of you," she said with a big grin on her face.

"I would do anything for you, my love." I planted a kiss on her lips. Mercedes got up, washed her face, brushed her teeth, and got back into bed before eating breakfast. I turned on the television, and we watched the news while she ate.

"Oh my God. I'm going to be late for work!" She said, now in a panic, kicking the covers off of her.

I grabbed her by the arm before she could get out of bed.

"No, you're not. I called your boss and told him you were not coming in this morning."

"You did what?"

"I called your boss. Today, you are all mine, and I am all yours. We are not getting out of this bed."

"Ooh, I love it when you take charge," she said, sliding back under the covers.

We stayed in bed all day, talking, making love, and watching television.

The next day, Mercedes went to work, and I went to Krystal Pharmacy. It was work as usual. Customers came in and out of the pharmacy with small white bags that had Krystal's printed in blue on the front of it. Some continued to their cars, and others would go next door to deal with a different type of pharmacist. This caused a problem. Moe owns the pharmacy, and he has tried to get help from the police, but some of them are on the drug dealer's payroll. I have often asked Moe why he was still there? His response is always the same. "I want to help people." If it weren't for Moe, a lot of them would have to go without their meds. He is very generous and does whatever he can for the people in the neighborhood.

If someone doesn't have enough money to pay for their medicine, he will credit them for the rest. Sometimes they paid him, but most of the time, he ended up writing it off. They couldn't pay him but had no problem paying the drug dealers in the abandoned house next door. I hated how they took advantage of Moe, but there was nothing I could do about that.

It was six o'clock when I walked into the house. Mercedes was cooking, and whatever it was smelled delicious. I walked into the kitchen, and there were barbecue ribs, macaroni and cheese, potato salad, and green beans on the table.

"Hello, my love." I wrapped my arms around her waist and kissed her.

"Dinner looks delicious, and I am starving."

"Well, have a seat, and I'll fix you some tea. The plates are on the table."

"How was your day?" I asked, scooping some mac and cheese on my plate.

"It was business as usual. And yours?"

"It was good, an easy day."

After dinner, we cuddled on the sofa and watched television. I must admit it felt really good holding her in my arms. When I'm with Mercedes, my world is calm. Nothing else matters. I can't imagine myself without her. She will most definitely be Mrs. Madison one day.

**Mercedes**

I must admit things were looking up for Richard and me. This past week has been fantastic. He kept his word and spent time with me, instead of working at the club. He has been so attentive and very romantic. I felt like I was on top of the world. I promised him I would try to be more understanding about his second job if he would cut back on his time at the club to maybe two nights a week. He agreed.

On Sunday, we went to church and saw Amanda and James there with Brianna. She's a beautiful baby. After service, the five of us went to eat at Sizzlers. When Richard and James went to fix their plates at the buffet, Amanda told me they were moving. She seemed surprised that I didn't know. She assumed Sharon had told me already. I explained to her that I haven't seen or heard from Sharon in a while. She seems to always be busy doing one thing or the other. Amanda confided in me that she felt like something was going on with Sharon when she and McKenzie visited them last week. She said she couldn't quite put her finger on it, but wanted me to see if I could talk to her. I told her I would. I also told her about my conversation with McKenzie.

"Amanda, do you think you could ask James to talk with McKenzie?"

"Honey, they have already talked. James won't tell me anything. That man can keep a secret."

"Well, so much for that."

We both nodded our heads in agreement. Richard and James came back to the table and the conversation continued to flow throughout our meal.

Once we finished dinner, we said our goodbyes and promised to get together before they left town. On the way home, I must have been pretty quiet.

"A penny for your thoughts," Richard said.

"I was just thinking about Sharon."

"What about her?"

"That's just it; I don't know. Amanda

said she didn't seem like herself when she was at their house a couple of weeks ago and thinks something is wrong."

"Maybe she just had a lot on her mind. That doesn't mean something is wrong."

"Yeah, you're probably right. I told Amanda I would give her a call to check on her.

"That sounds like a good idea."

**Sharon**

"What's up, girl?" Mercedes yelled into the phone.

"Nothing much, how have you been doing? I haven't seen or heard from you in a while."

"Girl, I'm doing fine. Things are looking up for Richard and me."

"That's good. I wish I could say the same about McKenzie and me."

"What's going on?"

"It's the same ole plot, and I know you think I'm petty, so there is no need going there."

"Sharon, if we were having this conversation before I got involved with Richard, you would be right. I would think you are petty, but now that I am with him, I fully understand where you are coming from."

"Oh, really now."

"Yes, Richard has been spending a lot of time at that club and not enough time at home."

"I thought you said things are looking up."

"I did. Let me finish. Last week, we talked, and he told me he was going to cut his hours working at the club to be with me. So now, instead of working four nights a week, he's only going to work two."

"At least the two of you could compromise. McKenzie is doing his own thing. I know he's working hard to prepare for our future, but he's destroying our marriage.  The sad part about it is he doesn't care."

"Sharon, he loves you, and you know it."

"Well, he's not showing it."

"Girl, you are crazy for even thinking that. He shows you by getting up working every day, providing for you, making sure that you want for nothing."

"See, that's where you're wrong. You think because he can buy and give me all the material things I want, everything should be okay? But what I want more than anything is his time and attention, which he is not providing."

"You're just going to have to sit him down and talk to him about it."

"Been there, done that. It hasn't changed a thing. So, the way I see it is if he won't spend time with me then, I'll find someone who will."

"You don't mean that."

"Oh, but I do, and I am."

"What about McKenzie?"

"What about him?"

"He's a good man, and you know it. This will break his heart."

"What about my heart? Every time he chooses work over me, that breaks my heart."

"Sharon, you will regret this. Don't do it. It's not worth it."

"I have to go. I'll think about it. Talk to you later.

"Byron, dinner was delicious," I said, finishing up the wonderful dinner he prepared.

"Why, thank you, Madam. I aim to please." He teased.

"I see you are a man of many talents."

"I try to be." He winked.

After dinner, we went into the living room and listened to some jazz. We talked and even danced. It felt great being in his arms.

"I could get used to this, you know," he said, looking into my eyes.

"I like this, too."

He lifted my chin and kissed me. My body began to tingle all over. The three glasses of wine didn't help either. I was as horny as hell.

He began kissing my neck and rubbing my breast. The next thing I knew, I was naked and screaming out his name. I was in  bliss until my cell phone rung.

"Hello," I answered.

"Hey babe, what are you doing?" McKenzie asked.

"I'm just sitting here, reading a book."

Byron watched me as I talked on the phone. He slipped his finger inside of me, and I bit my bottom lip to stop from gasping with pleasure.

"We just landed. I will call you back when I check-in and get settled at the hotel."

"Okay."

"I love you."

"I love you too, babe."

"Bye."

"Goodbye." I hung up the phone.

Byron pulled me close to him. "Im'ma give you what you love," he said seductively.

As I sat at the airport waiting for McKenzie to arrive, I couldn't help but think of Byron. These past few days have been out of this world. I wish we had more time to spend with each other. I was fantasizing about our rendezvous when McKenzie placed his hand on my shoulder startling me.

"Hey you," He said, planting a kiss on my cheek.

"How was your trip?"

"It was wonderful. I signed the contract."

"When do you start?"

"I told them in two weeks. I wanted to tie up some loose ends and make sure everything is to Byron's liking before I leave. Oh, I'm quite sure it is.

On the ride home, McKenzie told me all about the meeting, locations, and schedule. I tried to focus on him, but my mind kept going back to the last three days I had with Byron. I missed him terribly. I wanted to be in his arms. I looked at McKenzie and realized for the first time in a long time that I was falling out of love with him. This didn't come as a shock to me, because it was something I've been feeling for a long time now, and for once, I was honest with myself. Now, the question is, what do I do about it?

:: 77 ::

## McKenzie

"Since I came back from New York, Sharon has been very distant. Things between us are different. She won't talk to me. She won't let me touch her. We haven't made love since the day I came back from my business trip. She never has time for me. I know that sounds cliché, but I have been trying. I don't know what to do," McKenzie said, pouring his heart out to James.

"Man, you know she's been after you for a while about your job, and you were not spending time with her as she asked you to. So maybe, this is her way of getting back at you."

"Yeah, I thought about that too. But by now, she would have come around. I mean, it's been a week. I have to leave in another week to do the job. What am I supposed to do? I can't sit around and do nothing. I have to work."

"McKenzie, work isn't everything. You are very successful with your business. It's now time for you to start prioritizing things in your life. What's more important to you, your wife, or work?"

"My wife is the most important. After I complete this job, I'm going to cut back on my workload, spend more time with Sharon. Maybe have some babies." I said with a big grin on my face.

"Sounds like a plan to me, my brother."

I left for New York without even as much as a goodbye from Sharon. As a matter of fact, she was nowhere to be found. We had a huge argument last night, and she left. I called Mercedes and Amanda. Neither one of them had seen her. I drove all over town trying to find her.

I still don't understand why she got so upset when I told her I was going to send her a plane ticket to fly out to New York this weekend. I figured she would love to get away. I kept replaying that scene over and over again in my head.

"Babe, I'm going to buy you a plane ticket to New York for the weekend."

"I'm not flying anywhere."

"Why not?"

"If you want to be with me, then you come home. Other than that, I will not be at your beck and call, flying back and forth to New York to satisfy you."

"Sharon, I don't want to argue. I just figured you would enjoy getting away for the weekend."

"Well, you figured wrong. New York is your thing, not mine. You do what you have to do, Boo."

"What the hell does that mean? I'm working, not partying."

Sharon grabbed her keys and began walking toward the door.

"Sharon, can we talk about this?"

"I'm done talking."

"Where are you going?"

"I'm going to do me."

"You going to do you, so what does that mean?"

"It means, just what I said."


"Sir, fasten your seatbelt." The stewardess ordered. I was happy for the interruption. My mind was racing a mile a minute, trying to figure out what she meant by she's going to do her?

Once I got to New York and settled in my room, I tried calling her. There was no answer. I called Mercedes and asked her to go over to the house and check on Sharon for me. I told her about the argument last night without going into detail. I sure hope she can help her come to her senses because this is just crazy

## Mercedes

On Thursday, I decided to surprise Richard and take him out to lunch. As I waited at the traffic light, I noticed him getting into a silver BMW. On the front of the car was a personalized plate that had RENAE on it in bold black letters. My heart dropped. I couldn't believe it.

I decided to follow them. I don't know why it is, but whenever you are in a hurry, there is always some older person driving slowly in front of you. I saw them turn right on Crenshaw Blvd. I was now two blocks behind them and stopped at a traffic light. By the time I had gotten to Crenshaw, they were nowhere in sight. I circled a few blocks trying to find them. After not having any luck, I called my job and told them I needed the rest of the day off due to a family emergency. An emergency is exactly what it's going to be as soon as I get my hands on Richard.

He didn't come home last night. I had been up all night and gone through a bottle of wine waiting on him. I called out sick again the next morning.

"Mercedes, are you alright?" Mr. Randall asked.

"I'll be fine. I think I may be coming down with a stomach virus."

"Is there anything we can do for you?"

"No, sir, I think with some medicine and a lot of rest this weekend, I will be okay."

"Alright, you take care of yourself, and we will see you on Monday."

"Thank you. I'll see you on Monday. Goodbye."

"Goodbye."

Next, I called Sharon. No answer. I called Amanda.

"Hello."

"Hello, Amanda, how are you doing?"

"I'm doing great. I've been pretty busy packing."

"I know, I haven't been over there to help you pack, but I've been pretty busy myself lately."

"That's okay. I've been doing a little each day, so I'm almost done. I understand you have a job. I don't expect you to get off work and come over here to help me pack, especially when I'm home all day."

"I'm glad you understand, but that's no excuse."

"Well, girlfriend, trust me, I have no hard feelings."

"Thanks, but I will be there Saturday to help you finish packing. I promise."

Amanda and I talked for another hour about my situation with Richard. Well, I talked, and she mostly listened. It was like therapy, just talking about it. However, I still wondered about Richard and what this meant for our relationship, because one thing I was sure of, this was unacceptable, and I'm not putting up with it.

Around lunchtime, I headed back to the pharmacy. Richard's car was still in the parking lot.

When I walked into the store, there was an older man behind the counter. His name tag read Moe.

"Hello, can I help you?" He asked.

"Yes, I need to speak to Richard."

"No, Richard, works here."

"Excuse me, no Richard works here," I repeated.

"That's correct."

"Sir, my boyfriend's name is Richard Madison, and that is his car in your parking lot."

"Oh, that young man always parks there, but he doesn't work here."

I felt my blood boiling.

"Thank you, sir," I said as I walked out of the door.

Richard has been lying to me, and I'm going to get to the bottom of this. However, I couldn't stop wondering, what in the hell was he doing all day?

## Richard

Mmm, babe. I think it's time we get back.. I need to do some damage control."

"Just one more round before we go. You know it's been a while."

"I know, but Mercedes has been blowing up my phone," I said, referring to the twenty missed calls on my cell phone.

"Hey, she's waited these past two days. Surely, she can wait a few more hours. I want to be with you for a little longer."

I smiled and shook my head. "You know it is hard for me to resist you."

When I got home, Mercedes met me at the door with a large black garbage bag.

"Babe, what's going on?"

"What's going on is I want you to get out of my house."

"Just like that? You're not going to give me a chance to explain?"

"Oh, so you want a chance to explain. Well, explain this to me. Who the hell is Renae? And just what do you do for eight to ten hours a day, because you for damn sure don't work at Krystal Pharmacy. That's right, I went down there Friday to take you out to lunch and what do I see?" She continued, not giving me time to answer. "I see you getting into a BMW with a personalized plate that had Renae on it. So, I figured I would go home and wait for you there. But low and behold, you didn't come home. So, what do I do? I go back to Krystal's and come to find out, you don't work there. Now, you have the audacity to walk into my home and think you can tell me anything after staying out all weekend, without so much as a phone call."

She was throwing bags of my clothes out in the front yard.

"Babe, please don't do this."

"Do what? You brought this on yourself. Now, get your things and leave." She said, pointing to the bags in the yard.

"Okay, I'll leave. But let me tell you why I didn't come home this weekend," I said, trying to touch her, but she jerked away.

"Go ahead, tell me, so you can hurry up and go."

"Mercedes, I didn't come home, because Jimmy's mother was in the hospital and things didn't look good. Jimmy was in no shape to drive, so Renae offered to take him to Jersey to see his mother. I went along to help her drive.

His mother died two hours after we arrived. The funeral is Wednesday, and to answer your question, Renae works with us at the club. Nothing is going on between us."

"Why didn't you call me to let me know all this was going on?"

"I don't have an explanation for that. I was caught up in the situation at the moment. I was trying to console Jimmy. He'd just lost his mother. I figured I would deal with the rest later."

"Oh, deal with the rest later, meaning me?"

"Babe, I didn't mean it that way. It was just so much going on, and I just lost focus, that's all. I'm sorry, from the bottom of my heart, please forgive me."

I grabbed her hand and attempted to kiss it, but she snatched it away.

"Explain to me about your job. What have you been doing every day?"

"I've been working at the club. I would go in from ten in the morning until four o'clock in the afternoon for the happy hour crew. Mercedes, the truth is, I'm not a pharmacist, and I have never been. I lied because I didn't think a woman like you would give a guy like me a chance if I didn't have a nice paying job." I paused. She didn't say anything, so I continued. "I know I deceived you, but could you honestly stand there and tell me that if I had told you from the beginning that I was a bartender at a night club, you would have given me some face time?"

I could tell she was thinking about everything I was saying, and the look in her eyes confirmed it. She forgave me.

"The truth is Richard; you are probably right. More than likely, I wouldn't have given you a second thought. But now, you have my heart. I love you, but I'm not going to be your fool."

"Babe, I wouldn't do anything to hurt you. I love you." I pulled her into my arms.

"I love you, too."

Our love was sealed with a kiss. At that moment, I knew all was well again.

## Sharon

It was killing me not being able to see Byron all weekend because McKenzie was home. But when Byron emailed me on Sunday saying he wanted to be with me, I left the house while McKenzie was in the shower.

I know I was wrong for not telling him I was leaving, but I didn't want to have to come up with an excuse to go. It was better that way.

When I got to Byron's, he quickly opened the door and pulled me into his arms.

"Oh babe, I missed you," he said, kissing me as if his life depended on it.

"I missed you, too."

He led me to the bedroom. "I need you."

We made love off and on all day. I was on cloud nine until my cell phone rang. It was McKenzie. I chose not to answer it. I knew he would leave a message. I also knew he was going to be angry with me for leaving and not seeing him off. Honestly, I couldn't care less anymore. I don't love him the way a wife should love her husband. I would leave in a heartbeat, but Byron isn't singing the right tune just yet. So in the meantime, I'll have my cake and eat it, too.

I hadn't spoken to McKenzie for two days, so when he called me on Tuesday night, I answered the phone.

"Hello."

"Where the hell have you been? I have been calling you for days, and why haven't you returned my calls?" He said all in one breath, and with an attitude, I might add. I expected him to be angry, hell, I would've been surprised if he wasn't.

"You can talk to me better than that, and for your information, the phone line had to be repaired. I couldn't call out, and I couldn't get incoming calls."

"What about your cell phone?"

"I dropped it in the sink of dishwater while I was talking to Mercedes on Monday, and it was too late to get it changed out."

"Oh, you have an answer for everything I see."

"Whatever, McKenzie. Is this what you called me for?"

He sighed, and the tone of his voice softened.

"Sharon, what's going on with you?"

"What do you mean?"

"What's happening to us?"

"Nothing is happening to us. You are working all the time, so I am just coping and trying to find ways to occupy my time."

"And just how are you doing that?"

"What is this? Ask Sharon questions night?"

"No, I just feel like I'm losing you, and no matter how hard I try, nothing seems to make you happy anymore."

Let's talk about this when you come home."

"Yeah, maybe you're right. Get some rest, and I'll see you Saturday."

"Saturday?"

"Yeah, we're working all day Friday, so I'm flying out first thing Saturday morning."

"What time does your plane get in on Saturday?"

"It will be around ten-thirty."

"Okay, I'll see you then."

"You don't have to pick me up from the airport. I drove my car."

"Oh, that's right."

"Sharon."

"Yes."

"I love you."

"Me too, Good night."

"Good night."

## Mercedes

Things were back to normal. I returned to work, and Richard was working at the club.

He was telling me the truth about Jimmy's mother. We attended her funeral, and on the drive home, we had a heart to heart discussion about our relationship and where it was going. All in all, things seem to be looking up once again. He asked me to marry him, and I accepted. I know we have a lot of things to work out. For me, it's the trust factor. I'm still struggling with that. I love him, God knows I do. I'm trying very hard not to doubt him, especially after this last episode with him not coming home all weekend or calling. I'm going to take it one day at a time.

My mother seems to think I feel the way I do because I have seen how my brother's treated their girlfriends in the past. She's probably right. I never understood how those women could be so naïve.

I promised myself I would never let a man play me for a fool, and I meant it.

When I came back from lunch, there were a dozen roses on my desk. The card read:

TO THE LOVE OF MY LIFE, JUST BECAUSE…

LOVE, RICHARD.

"Hey, you," I said when Richard answered the phone.

"Hey, what's up?"

"I' m calling to say thank you for the roses. They are lovely."

"You're welcome, anything for you, babe."

"Thanks."

"I will see you when I get home tonight."

"Okay. Hey Richard," I said right before he hung up

"Yes."

"I love you."

"I love you too, babe."

Part Two:

# A Storm Is Coming

## Sharon

Oh no, not again. I sat on the side of the bathtub in disbelief. The pregnancy test was positive. I have been so careful not to make the same mistake. I don't understand what went wrong. Tears began to roll down my face. Then the realization hit. Oh God, I don't even know who the father is. I can't have this baby. I started sobbing. After I finished having my meltdown, I threw away all evidence of the pregnancy test and got myself together.

I was meeting McKenzie for lunch at Antonio's and couldn't let him see me in this mental state. Things were getting better between us. He had lightened his workload tremendously since he finished the project in New York. We had a heart to heart talk about our present situation and our future. Of course, he mentioned children, and I agreed to have at least one, but I told him I didn't know when I would be ready. He said he could accept that and was happy the answer wasn't no.

I called the Women's Choice Clinic, and they had an opening today at three o'clock. I told the receptionist to put me down for that appointment.

When I arrived at Antonio's, McKenzie was waiting for me by the entrance door. He kissed me, and we went inside the restaurant.

After we were seated, the waitress came over and took our order.

"Sharon, I've been thinking. How would you feel about us spending Christmas with Amanda and James in Atlanta?"

"Oh, I would love it! That's a great idea! Can we invite Mercedes and Richard to come along?"

"Sounds good to me. You ask Mercedes, and I'll talk with James to see if it will be a good time for us to visit."

"Okay."

After we finished our meals and said our goodbyes, my next stop was the Women's Choice Clinic.

On my way there, I called Mercedes and told her about the plans to visit Amanda and James. She was excited and asked me to call her with the details.

I pulled into the clinic's parking lot. Not wanting to chance someone seeing my car, I parked around the back of the building.

I followed the same routine as I did before. While waiting to be called to the back, I noticed this young lady staring at me. The way she was looking at me made me feel uncomfortable. Finally, I asked.

"Excuse me, have we met?"

"No."

"Then why do you keep staring at me?"

"These are my eyes, and I can look at who I want to look at," she said, as she rolled her neck and smacked her lips.

"Little girl, this ain't what you want!" I smiled and decided to take the adult approach.

"You are correct. Those are your eyes, but it's not polite to stare."

"It's not polite to be in here killing your baby either, but you're doing it," she retorted.

"What I do is none of your business!" I stood ready for battle. Little did she know, she had struck a nerve. "Let me tell you something, little girl."

The receptionist came from behind the counter and stood between us.

"Ladies, I need the two of you to calm down."

"Ma'am, I don't know what her problem is. She started with me. I hadn't said anything to her."

She was trying to look all innocent.

The receptionist looked at me, then at her. "If there are any more outbursts, both of you will have to leave. Is that understood?"

"Yes," I said and sat back down.

The young woman looked at me with a smirk on her face.

Shortly after that, the nurse called me to the back.

"Monique Smith."

I got up and followed her.

"Hmmm," the young lady said, as I walked passed her.

The nurse led me to the room where I had to look at the abortion video again, but I wasn't interested in the video. I was puzzled by the young lady in the lobby. Suddenly, I recognized who she was, and a cold chill came over me. I was so deep in thought that I didn't notice the video was over until the nurse came in to take me to the exam room. She handed me a cup for a urine sample.

A few minutes later, Nurse Samantha came in. She looked down at my chart.

"Ah, I remember you, Ms. Smith."

"Yes, and I remember you too, Ms. Samantha," I said, with a hint of sarcasm.

She smiled.

"Well, let's get started, shall we?"

"Yes." I nodded.

"Monique, you are pregnant," she announced. She didn't wait for a response. She just continued with her list of questions. But, when she asked me did I know who the father was, I honestly didn't know. Although McKenzie and I were working on our relationship, I still hadn't let Byron go, so I most definitely knew I couldn't have this baby.

I made it home before McKenzie. I went upstairs, undress, and got into bed. I was still drowsy from the anesthesia and must have been sleeping hard because I didn't hear McKenzie when he came in from work. I also didn't hear the phone ring when the nurse called to check on me.

I woke up and went downstairs. McKenzie was sitting on the couch watching television.

"Hi," I said when I entered the living room. "Why didn't you wake me up when you got home?"

"You were resting so peacefully. I didn't want to bother you."

With a look of concern on his face, he asked, "Sharon, are you alright?"

"Yes, I'm fine. Why do you ask that?"

"A nurse called from Dr. Freil's office. She left a message on the answering machine."

"What did she say?" I asked, trying not to sound as nervous as I was.

"She said she was calling to see if you were doing okay."

I couldn't believe I missed that call. Thank God for small miracles.

My mind was racing for something to say. Finally, I said.

"I was having bad stomach cramps and throwing up after lunch, so I went to the doctor to get checked for food poisoning."

"Are you feeling better?"

"Yes, I am. The doctor gave me some antibiotics, which made me sleepy, but I'm okay."

He pulled me down on his lap and kissed me on my forehead. We spent the rest of the evening cuddling on the couch.

The next couple of weeks went by like a breeze. McKenzie didn't suspect a thing, probably because he was finishing up a small project before we headed out of town. That job couldn't have come at a better time.

Rhayne

## McKenzie

"Sharon has been acting strange. Well, I wouldn't say strange but different. She is reverting to her old ways. I thought we had gotten past all of that, but I guess not. I just have this feeling that something is not right. This is why I called you today, Mr. Everette. I want you to follow my wife. Find out what she's been up to."

"I'll get right on it, Mr. Taylor. Do you have a picture of her on hand?"

"Yes." McKenzie pulled a photo of Sharon out of his desk drawer.

"I also need you to tell me about her habits? What kind of vehicle does she drive? Your address and any other information you think may be helpful in this investigation."

"She drives a candy apple red Jaguar. As for her habits, I'm really not sure these days. I'm usually gone in the morning before she awakes, and when I get home, most of the time, she is not there."

"Does she tell you where she's been?"

"Mainly, she says she's out with her friends. I only know of one best friend she has living here, and she works during the day."

"Well, what's her name, and where does she work?"

"Mercedes Wilkerson. She works at James and Randall Law Firm."

"Any other persons she has mentioned lately?"

"I can't think of anyone else."

"Okay, I'll start with this, and if you think of someone or something later, give me a call."

"I will."

"Thank you, Mr. Everette."

"Call me, Harold."

"Okay, thank you, Harold, and you can call me McKenzie."

"Yes, sir." He stood to leave.

"You know, Harold, you came highly recommended by a friend of mine."

"That's great. If you don't mind me asking, what's your friend's name?"

"Travis Wynn, he's my frat brother."

"Oh yes, I remember Mr. Wynn. How is he doing?"

"He' s doing great. He has a new wife and a new baby."

"You don't say. The next time you speak to him, tell him I said hello."

"I will. So tell me how soon can you get started?"

"I can start in the morning. What time do you leave for work?"

"I leave around seven-thirty."

"I will be there, but you will not see me. Just know, I'll be on the job. I don't want to blow my cover." He winked.

"I understand. By the way, we will be leaving Saturday going to Atlanta to visit some friends. We will be back on the second of January."

"That's fine. I'll just pick up where I left off when you return." We shook hands once more, and Harold left my office. I called Sharon. No answer. I knew Mercedes was working, but I called her anyway.

"Hello, James and Randall's office, Mercedes speaking."

"Hi, Mercedes, this is McKenzie."

"Oh, hi. What's going on?"

"Nothing much. I was wondering if you have heard from my wife today. I've been calling her, but she's not answering her cell phone or the house phone."

"No, I haven't spoken with her today, but if she calls, I will tell her to give you a call."

"Thanks, I appreciate it."

"So, are you and Richard ready for the trip?"

"Yes, I am counting down the days."

"Me too," I chuckled.

"I am so ready to see Amanda."

"I know what you mean. I'm ready to see my boy James, too. However, I am very excited about getting to see my god-baby."

"I just bet you are." Mercedes laughed. "You will probably have her on your hip the entire time we're there."

"You're probably right."

We both laughed.

"Well, I have to get back to work," she said.

"No problem. I'll talk to you later."

"Goodbye."

"Goodbye."

After hanging up with Mercedes, I tried to get some work done. I was having a hard time concentrating. I kept asking myself, do I really want to know what my wife is doing? People always say, 'Be careful what you ask for.' I just hope I'm wrong about this.

## Mercedes

'Sorry I missed your call. Leave a brief message, and I'll get back to you.' Sharon's voice chimed on the other end of the line. Hmm, I wonder what's up with her.

When I talked to McKenzie earlier, he seemed a little agitated. I'll make a mental note to call her again later and find out what she's been up to.

Today was pretty busy for a Wednesday at the firm, so when it was five o'clock, I was more than happy to be leaving for the day. Before heading home, I stopped by Riley's to pick up something for dinner. Just as I parked the car, my phone rang.

"Hey, babe."

"Hi."

"I was calling to tell you I'm going to be home late tonight. D said he needed me to stay over for a while. Jimmy called out sick."

"Okay, do you want me to bring you some dinner? I just pulled in to Riley's to pick us up something to eat."

"No. I'll just grab something from the kitchen here. Besides, I told you I didn't want you coming down to this part of town."

"Yeah, I know."

"You know I'm only trying to protect you, babe."

"Protect me from what?"

"Mercedes don't do this. I'm not going to get into it with you right now. I'll see you when I get home."

Oh no, he didn't! Who the hell does he think he is? I ranted to myself.

I was just about to call Richard back when I saw Sharon across the street coming out of Lagoon's Steakhouse. She was not alone.

She was with this tall, handsome man. I wonder who he is? As quick as that thought crossed my mind, it didn't take long for me to find out, because they were at the driver's side of her car kissing, very intimately.

I gasped. Oh my God, she's having an affair. I blinked in disbelief. I couldn't believe she went through with it.

"Hello."

"Amanda, this is Mercedes."

"Hi, girlfriend, how are you?"

"I'm fine, but you won't believe what I'm about to tell you."

"What?" Amanda asked, waiting in suspense.

"Sharon is having an affair!" I yelled into the phone.

"She's what?"

"She's cheating on McKenzie! I'm sitting here in Riley's parking lot watching her tongue down this man."

"Mercedes, you are kidding me, right?"

"Do you honestly think I would call you and joke about something like this, Amanda?"

"Wait! I thought things were alright between those two."

"I did too, but I guess not. Today, McKenzie called me looking for her; I thought she might have been out shopping or something."

"So, what are they doing now?"

"They are laughing."

"I can't believe she would do something like this."

"Me either and in broad daylight, too. But I do remember her telling me she was going to do her because she was tired of being alone."

"Oh my God. You know this is just going to tear McKenzie to pieces when he finds out about this."

"Amanda, you cannot tell James. You know he will tell McKenzie."

"I know. What do you suppose we do about this?"

"We aren't going to do anything about this. Sharon is a grown woman, and if she wants to risk losing everything for this man, then more power to her. She deserves whatever happens to her."

"Maybe we should talk to her."

"Talk to her for what? So she can tell us to mind our own business? I'm not saying anything to her."

"I guess you're right. What's done in the dark will come to light, eventually."

"That's right, and when McKenzie finds out about this, she can't blame it on us. Girl, they are backing out of the parking lot."

"Are they together?"

"No. They are in separate cars. They are going opposite directions."

"You know that really pisses me off because McKenzie is a good man, and he doesn't deserve this."

"I know. I know." I agreed. "But there is nothing we can do about it. I'll call you later."

"Okay, call me sooner if you find out anything more."

"I will, with your nosey self."

We both laughed and ended the call.

## Richard

"I'm sorry, I'm late," I said, through the kisses. "I had to lie to my girl to buy us some time."

"I missed you."

"I missed you, too. Let's stop all of this talking, and let me give you what you came here for."

"Oh yeah, but first, I need to take a shower."

"Go ahead. There are some clean towels and washcloths on my bed."

As I held my head under the water rinsing the shampoo from out of my hair, I heard the shower curtain open and close—the feel of soft lips covering my wood, and teasing its head. Before I knew it, I had exploded.

I quickly turned off the water. "Let's take this party to the bedroom," I said, stepping out of the shower.


It was late when I got home. Mercedes was wide awake.

"Hey." I leaned over to kiss her, and she turned her head.

"Don't hey me. I thought you said you were going to work for a little while longer, not all night."

"I did, but there was no one else there to work the bar."

"Whatever. I'm not going to argue with you tonight. I'm tired."

I looked over on her nightstand. Thank God for wine. I jumped in the shower. When I returned to bed, Mercedes was fast asleep. Snoring, I might add. I went downstairs to watch television. I noticed a rose on the coffee table with a little note attached. It read: Hey, handsome. There's a treat for you on the top floor. I smiled. Now I know why she was a little salty. I'll have to make it up to her later.

I awoke earlier than Mercedes the next morning. I went downstairs and made her a delicious breakfast of eggs, bacon, blueberry pancakes, a bowl of sliced strawberries, and orange juice. I was hoping this little gesture would get me out of the dog house. But when Mercedes came downstairs, she looked at the table and walked out of the kitchen.

"Mercedes, what's wrong? You're not hungry?"

"You know, every time I get angry with you, you seem to think all you have to do is cook me a meal, send me flowers, or say all the sweet little things you think I want to hear and everything will be alright. Well, not this time, sweetheart. So, you enjoy your breakfast this morning. I have to get to work."

And like that, she walked out of the front door. She was really angry.

I decided I was going to have to do something very special to get her to come around, and what better way to say I'm sorry than a nice pair of diamond earrings.

"Hello sir, may I help you," the small petite woman asked, standing behind the jewelry case.

"Yes, I'm looking for a nice pair of diamond earrings for my girlfriend."

"Oh, how nice. Come this way. Let me show you our selection." She walked over to one of the jewelry cases with earrings in it. "Here is a nice pair of half hoop earrings."

They were gold and trimmed with diamonds.

"These look nice but let me see those over there," I said, pointing to the earrings on the right side of the case.

"Ah, these are very lovely." She put the earrings on top of the glass case so that I could get a better look at them.

"I think these are the ones."

She nodded. "You've made a great choice. Do you want them wrapped?"

"Yes, please." I had chosen a pair of one-carat diamond platinum studs.

"That will be $1,500, sir."

I pulled out my credit card, and she swiped it on the machine. It showed purchase approved. She handed me the receipt, and I signed it. She wrapped the earrings, and I was on my way.

This was the perfect gift. There is no way Mercedes will stay mad with me once she sees everything I have planned for her tonight.

**Mercedes**

"Hello."

"Hi, it's me, Mercedes."

"I know who you are."

"Girl, I need to talk to you. Are you busy?"

"No, I was just about to pour me up a cup of coffee."

"Okay; well, listen while you pour your coffee because I really need to vent about Richard.

"What has he done now?"

"I believe he's cheating on me. He's been staying out late, and when he comes home, he heads right for the shower."

"Well, have you asked him?"

"Ask him for what? He's only going to deny it."

"True, so, what's his excuse for coming home late?"

"He claims he's working at the club."

"Okay, well, the next time he tells you he's working at the club, go there and see if he's there."

"I thought about that already. But you know, I'm afraid to go by myself because he said it's located in a rough area."

"Mercedes, men will tell you anything to keep you from finding out the truth."

"So, you think I should go?"

"What do you think? If you really want to know, then go."

"You know what, I'm going to do it. And if he is cheating, it's over. Will you go with me?"

"Sure, when do you want to go?"

"Let's go after our trip to Atlanta. I don't want to spoil my vacation."

"I hear you, girl. We don't need to be acting like fools away from home."

"Okay, you are right about that."

Sharon and I continued to talk for another fifteen minutes as I caught her up on everything that happened between Richard and me. I have to admit it felt good getting all of that off my chest.

I thought about what she said and decided that during my lunch hour, I would try to find Club Gemini. When I got to the office, I sat down at my desk and began to search for the club's location.

To my surprise, there was no address, but there was a phone number. Right before leaving for lunch, I called the club.

"Club Gemini," the man answered on the other end of the line.

"Hello, my girls and I would like to check out your club, but we don't have the location."

"We're at 321 Bartowe St."

"321 Bartowe St," I repeated back to the guy.

"Yes, do you know where Bartowe St is."

"Yes, thank you." I hung up the phone.

I hurried out of the office and drove to the location. It was only five miles away from

Geri's heading towards the other side of town.

It's ppposite the side of town, I stay on, which is why I never go that way. One thing is for sure. It's not in a rough area.

Club Gemini is a plain white building with dark tinted windows. On the front of the building is a large black sign with GEMINI in big, bold gold letters. There were four cars in the parking lot. None of them belonged to Richard. I found that to be odd because he's always saying he had to be there early to help get things set up, but that's okay. Now that I know where the club is, I will most definitely be making an appearance.

## Sharon

After talking with Mercedes, I decided I would do some last-minute shopping, so I hurried and took a shower. As I was getting dressed, my cell phone rang. I looked at the small window on the front of the phone that identifies the caller. It was McKenzie.

"Hello."

"Hey babe, I see you're up."

"Yeah, I was just getting dressed. I figured I'd go do some last-minute shopping."

"Okay, sounds good. I was calling to hear your voice. I wish I were home right now. The things I would love to do to you."

"Well, I would have to pass on that anyway. I need to get some shopping done before we leave."

"In that case, Mrs. Taylor, do you think you could find time to have lunch with me later?

"I don't know. I'll call you, okay." I hung up the phone before he could protest.

On my way downstairs, the doorbell rang.

"Who is it?" I said, opening the door.

"It's UPS, ma'am. I have a package for Sharon Taylor."

"I'm Sharon."

He handed me the box and had me sign the electronic device confirming I had received the package.

"I hope you have a Merry Christmas, ma'am," he said as he walked down the porch steps.

"You, too."

The package was from McKenzie so I decided to open it later. I locked the door behind me and headed to Byron's house. I changed my mind about shopping. I needed some of Byron's TLC instead.

"I hope you haven't eaten because I have prepared breakfast for us." He led the way to the kitchen.

"No, I haven't. I was too excited about seeing you," I smiled.

"The feeling is mutual."

There were blueberry muffins, sausage links, fruit salad made with cantaloupe, honeydew, pineapple, and grapes and freshly squeezed orange on the table.

"Sweetheart, this is lovely."

"It's all for you."


After breakfast, we cleared the table and cleaned the kitchen.

While I washed dishes, he stepped behind me, wrapping his arms around my waist, planting small kisses on my neck.

"You know I love you, don't you?" He said.

"Yes, and I love you, too."

"Sharon turn around."

Byron stepped back, giving me space to turn.

When I turned around, he was holding a small box wrapped in red paper with a silver bow on top.

"What is this?"

"Open it."

I hurried and opened the box. Inside was a beautiful gold ring with a huge pink diamond in the center, and small diamonds on each side of the band.

"Oh, Byron, it's beautiful!"

"Just like the woman I bought it for."

"You always say the right things." I blushed.

"And I mean every bit of it."

"I have something for you, too."

"Sharon, I told you, you didn't have to get me anything."

"I know, but I wanted to."

I grabbed my purse and pulled out a long black box with a gold bow and handed it to him.

He opened the box. "Babe, this is a nice watch."

"I had it custom made for you." I beamed.

The gift was a Rolex. It had a gold facing. The roman numbers were made out of diamonds. The band was gold, and Byron's name was embroidered in the center of it.

Byron smiled. "Let's take this upstairs."

"I concur," I said as I followed him upstairs to his bedroom where he showed me just how much he missed me.

We made love for the next two hours and fell asleep in each other's arms. When I awakened and looked at the clock on the nightstand, it was two-thirty. I jumped up and startled Byron.

"Babe, what's wrong?" He asked, sitting up in bed.

"I have to get home before McKenzie gets there. He's been complaining about me not being home when he gets in from work, and I'm running out of excuses."

"Well, tell him the truth."

"I can't do that."

"Why not? I'll take care of you."

I stopped and looked at him. "Are you serious?"

"I'm not joking. I want you here with me."

"Why now?"

"I love you, Sharon, and it drives me crazy knowing that every time you leave me, you're going home to him."

"What about Renae?"

"What about Renae? She would be gone in a heartbeat. Will you stay?"

"Will I what?"

"Sharon, don't play with me, will you stay?"

"Byron, you just can't spring all of this on me and expect me to just say yes."

"Why not, you love me, don't you?"

"Yes, but."

"But what? I'm only good enough for you as a part-time lover."

"Babe, please don't do this to me, not right now. I need time to think."

"Think about what? You've been talking about how you wish we were together, and now you have to think about it?"

I could sense Byron was getting angry.

"Sweetheart, all I'm saying is right now is not a good time for me to decide anything. I'm getting ready to go on this trip in two days. I just need time to digest it all. When I come back, I will have an answer for you, I promise."

"Alright, I'll give you that time, but when you come back, I want an answer."

"Okay." I kissed him goodbye and left.

## Mercedes

The trip to Atlanta was wonderful. It was great seeing Amanda and James. Brianna had really grown, and she was so beautiful.

The time away did us all some good, and there was no drama.  Now that we were back, things have gotten worst. So, I decided to pick up where I left off and find out what Richard's been up to which is why I paid McKenzie a visit.

"Hello, Ms. Sylvia," I said, walking into his office and closing the door.

"Hello, Ms. Wilkerson."

"Is McKenzie busy?"

"Hold on a minute, and I'll see if he's available.

"Mr. Taylor, Ms. Wilkerson, is here to see you."

"Send her in." McKenzie's voice hovered over the intercom.

"Go on in, dear." Sylvia pointed to McKenzie's office door.

"Thank you."

When I entered McKenzie's office, he was sitting at his desk, looking through a stack of papers.

"Hello," I said, as I approached his desk.

"Hey, what brings you by?"

"Well, I have a big favor to ask. I would have called, but I wanted to ask you this in person." I sat down in one of the two chairs in front of his desk.

He walked from around his desk and sat in the chair next to me.

"So, what's the favor?"

"I want you to go with me to Club Gemini."

He eyed me suspiciously but didn't say a word, so I felt the need to say more.

"You know what I've been going through with Richard. Well, I think it's time I get to the bottom of it so that I can move on with my life, one way or the other, depending on the outcome."

"I understand, but are you sure you want to do this?

"No, I'm not sure," I smiled weakly. "But I do know I'm about to lose my mind with all of this wondering. I can't take it any more."

He sighed. "Okay, so when do you want to go?"

"What about Friday night?"

"Friday night," he pondered. "Friday is good."

"Thanks." I stood to leave and gave him a hug.

"I will call you later so we can make arrangements."

"Sounds great. I'll see you Friday, and I will be waiting on your call," he smiled.

I left McKenzie's office hopeful that I would finally get some answers, but nervous about what I might discover.

## Sharon

"Hello. Yes, I know. I miss you, too, babe. Okay, I'm on my way. I should be there in fifteen minutes. Yes, I'm ready. Uh, huh, I'm only wearing my trench coat," I purred into the phone.

I was on my way to the hotel to meet Byron. It was the first time I've gotten to be with him since we came back from Atlanta. Not that I didn't try, but he was away on business.

When I pulled up to the hotel, the valet attendant took my keys.

"Do you have any bags, ma'am?" The doorman asked.

"No," I said, walking up the stairs.

He hurriedly ran up the stairs in front of me and opened the door. I got to the room and knocked on the door. Byron opened it quickly and pulled me into his arms, kissing me like he was a starved lion, and his life depended on me for survival.

Three and a half hours later, I was walking out of the hotel on his arm.

On the way home, I reminisced about our time together. Everything was just perfect. We made love over and over again. I could still feel his touch and smell his scent all over me.

Although I must say I was relieved he didn't mention about me leaving McKenzie and moving in with him. A part of me was sad that he didn't.

I pulled in the driveway and began to panic. What the hell is he doing home so early? Think Sharon, Think!

McKenzie was getting his briefcase out of his car. I sat there watching him. I needed to come up with a good lie and quick.

He started walking towards my car. I would have sworn I could hear my heart beating through my chest.

"Hey babe, how are you doing?" He asked, opening my car door.

"Where have you been like that?" He asked as he scanned my attire or lack thereof.

"I went by your office to surprise you."

"Did you now?" He looked skeptical.

"Yes, really, but Sylvia told me you  left for the day, and so I hurried home in hopes of beating you here so that I could be waiting for you upstairs.

"Well, let me see my surprise."

I stepped out of the car and opened my trench coat.

"Wow!"

I wrapped my arms around his neck and planted a kiss on his cheek.

"That would have been a wonderful surprise, babe, but I have a lot of paperwork to do right now, so I'll have to make it up to you later."

"That's okay." I tried to sound disappointed, but the truth is I didn't want to have sex with McKenzie.

Besides, with the soreness between my thighs from my rendezvous with Byron, I didn't think I could've handled it anyway.

I walked inside the house, took a warm bath, climbed in bed between the sheets, and drifted off to sleep.

## McKenzie

Any doubt I had about her cheating on me was confirmed. I know she's cheating. She must think I'm stupid. Now, I must admit the lie she told about going to the office would've been convincing if Sylvia were there. But, Sylvia needed to leave after lunch to handle personal business.

I also left early to spend time with Sharon, only

to find her not home when I got there. Then she had the nerve to be wearing only a trench coat. The dead giveaway was the wetness between her thighs, not to mention the smell of men's cologne, which by the way, wasn't mine. She walked into the house and went straight to the bathroom to shower. I was hurt, but I kept my cool. Hopefully, Harold will have some information for me soon.

## Mercedes

When I got home from work to my surprise, Richard was there and had cooked dinner. As we sat across the table from each other, I couldn't keep my eyes off him. He looked up from his plate and caught me staring at him.

"Why are you looking at me like that?"

"Who is she, Richard?"

"Who is she? Babe, what are you talking about?"

"Oh, you dumb now, huh, or do you think I'm just stupid!

"Mercedes, you need to stop this. I have told you over and over again. There is no other woman. I love you, and you are all I need."

"Yeah, you can sell it, but I'm not buying it. I'm not a fool, honey. You're not having sex with me, so I know there has to be someone else."

My eyes begin to fill with tears, but I refused to let him see me cry. I had promised myself that I wouldn't shed another tear over him, and I was going to keep that promise come hell or high water.

"Babe, I'm not cheating on you." He said, walking over to me and placing his hand on my back.

"Don't touch me."

"You know what Mercedes, I'm getting tired of this. All I wanted to do was have a nice, quiet evening with you, but obviously, all you want to do is argue. I'M DONE!" He walked out of the kitchen and into the living room. He grabbed his jacket off the coat stand and walked out of the door.

I didn't move from my seat until I heard his car pulling out of the driveway, for fear I would beg him to stay. After he left, I ran to the bedroom, lay across the bed, and cried.

## Richard

"Hey, I need to see you. I'll be there in twenty minutes."

I turned on the radio in my car. Secret Lovers by Atlantic Star was playing. I turned up the volume and sang along as I thought about how on point the lyrics were.

I thought about Mercedes and the argument we just had but quickly dismissed it after I pulled up to the beautiful two-story brick home. I got out of the car, walked up to the front door, and rang the doorbell.

"Hey."

"Hey, come on in."

"Thanks. I just want to say I appreciate you taking this time to see me. I know we don't get to see each other often, but I love it when we do."

"Yeah, I do, too."

"Well, that's about to change soon."

"Really, what's up?"

"Mercedes tripping, and I'm sick and tired of going through this."

"So, what are you going to do about it?"

"I'm still debating on that."

"If you have to think about it, then you're not done."

"Look, I didn't come over here to get in an argument with you, too. I just need you right now; all of you." I was irritated and didn't need any more drama. "Let's just enjoy each other's company, okay?"

"Okay, if it's all of me you want, then all of me you shall have because I aim to please you, babe."

"I can't believe it's three in the morning. Mercedes is going to be mad as hell."

"Then, don't go."

"I can't stay," I started getting dressed.

"You can't or you won't."

"Both. I have to go home. Things are already complicated. Plus, you're seeing someone too, so don't act like you would be available if I broke things off with her right now."

"I've been thinking about that."

"You have?"

"Yes, I have. I'm happy when I'm with you, so I've considered ending that relationship. But, I need to know that you are ready to be mine and mine only."

"Of course, I am. I've been waiting on you to want to be with me exclusively. All this sneaking around is wearing me out. You just say the word, and I will drop Mercedes like a bad habit."

"Okay, well, let me end mine first, and I'll let you know when you can move in."

"No joke, don't be playing with me now."

"I'm not playing, just give me some time."

"Okay."

On the way home, I rehearsed the lie I was going to tell Mercedes. I knew it was going to take a lot of begging to get her to forgive me this time, but a part of me didn't care. I just needed to buy some time until I could move out.

As I drove into the driveway, I noticed her car was not in the garage. On the refrigerator, under a grape magnet, was a folded piece of paper with Richard in big letters on it. I removed the note and sat down at the counter and opened it.

Richard,

I've gone to my parents. I need to clear my head. I don't know when I will return, but I believe this time apart will do us some good. I will call you later.

Mercedes.

I breathed a sigh of relief. At least I know she's okay, and most importantly, she hadn't kicked me out of the house yet. I started to call her but opted to let her call me first. I left the note on the counter and went upstairs to go to bed.

Part Three:

# It All Comes Tumbling Down

**Mercedes**

I checked into a hotel. I didn't want to be around Richard. As a matter-of-fact, I don't want to even look at him right now.

"I have had enough. I'm at the point where I don't care if he's cheating or not. He has to go. He's no good for me. I can't keep living my life like this. I know I can do better than him, and I deserve better." I said between sobs to Amanda.

"You're right, honey. If he can't treat you the way you deserve to be treated, then I say let him go."

"I am. I know I can do better."

"So, what are you going to do?"

"First, I'm going to find out about this job of his. McKenzie and I are going to Club Gemini this Friday. But since that's a couple of days away, and he thinks I'm at my parents. I'm going to do a little investigating on my own. So, in the morning, I will be renting a car and following him around," I said between sniffs.

"I think that's a good idea," she agreed. "You be careful, okay?"

"I will."

I could hear the baby crying in the background.

"Mercedes, let me call you back. It's Brianna's feeding time."

"You don't have to call me back. It's late. I'll talk to you later. Thanks for listening."

"No problem, but call me if you need to talk, okay?"

"I will."

"Love you, my sister."

"Love you, too."

"Good night."

"Good night."

I walked into the bathroom and turned on the shower, setting its temperature as hot as I could stand it. I undressed and stepped under the water. When the hot water touched my body, all of the tension I had begun to rinse away.

As I lathered my body, I thought of how I was going to put my plan into action. I knew Richard wouldn't get up until around noon, because that's what he usually does, being that he has to work late every night, or so he says.

I figured I would get up first thing in the morning and rent a car from Enterprise. Then, I would park down the street from my house, just far enough where I can see the garage and wait for him to leave.

After rinsing off, I got out of the shower, wrapped the teri-cloth robe around my wet body, put on my nightgown, and climbed into bed.

I tried to sleep but couldn't, so I decided to watch television. I settled on watching the rerun of the Jeffersons.

I wondered what Richard was doing. I looked over at the clock on the nightstand. It was three o'clock in the morning. I have got to get some sleep.

I set the alarm for eight o'clock and turned off the television. I don't know what time I finally dozed off, but it didn't seem very long before the alarm awakened me. I hit the snooze button and rolled out of bed. Forty-five minutes later, I was dressed and walking out of the hotel.

The drive to Enterprise was about ten minutes away. I turned on the radio and "Take a Bow" by Rhianna was playing. The lyrics made me feel as though I was preparing for battle; as if I were getting my mind right to kick him to the curve.

When I arrived at Enterprise, there was this little old lady behind the counter. I just knew it was going to take forever, but to my surprise, it wasn't long at all. That's why they say, "Don't judge a book by its cover."

Twenty minutes after I arrived, I was pulling out of the parking lot in a green Toyota Corolla with tinted windows.

Before heading to my house, I stopped at a convenience store and bought myself some snacks. I went to McDonald's to grab some breakfast, and then, I was on my way.

Once on my street, I parked three houses down behind Mr. Brady's truck. As soon as I turned the engine off, Mr. Brady walked out of his house. I waved at him as he walked towards the car.

Mr. Brady is an older man. He and his wife have been living in the neighborhood for years. They are sweet people and often look out for me. They're like my adopted grandparents.

"Good morning, young lady, I didn't know who you were in this car."

"Good morning Mr. Brady, how are you?"

"Oh, I'm getting along fine, what about yourself?"

"I'm okay. If you don't mind, can I sit here in front of your house for a while?"

"Oh no, I don't mind at all. If you don't mind me asking, what's going on?" He asked, looking at me intently.

"I just need to watch my house for a little bit."

"Did something happen?"

"I really don't want to talk about it right now," I said, with a hint of sadness in my voice.

"I understand. If you need anything, come knock on the door."

"I will. Thanks, Mr. Brady."

He nodded his head.

"Mercedes."

"Sir."

"I know it's none of my business, but you know I love you like you are one of my own, so I'm a say this and leave you alone."

I listened.

"If you can't trust him, then you don't need to be with him."

"Yes, sir," I said, holding my head down.

He patted the door and walked away.

Meanwhile, I prepared myself for whatever the day may bring.

## Richard

I was awakened out of a deep sleep by the phone ringing. I figured it might have been Mercedes, so I quickly picked it up.

"Hello."

"Good morning."

"Good morning. When are you coming home?"

"I don't know, didn't you get my letter?" She responded with agitation.

"Yeah, I got it, and I think we need to talk, don't you?"

"I do, but right now, I have a lot to think about."

"You know I love you, right?"

"Uh-huh, well, I got to go jump in the shower. Mom and I are going to run some errands this morning. I just wanted you to know I made it safe."

"Okay, I'll call you later."

"Bye." She hung up the phone.

I know she's still angry about last night, but she'll get over it.

"Hello."

"What are you doing?"

"Nothing. I took the week off, remember?"

"I need to see you."

"When?"

"As soon as possible."

"Okay, where do you want to meet?"

"At my house."

"At your house, are you crazy?"

"Yes, I'm crazy about you," I said naughtily.

"You know what I mean."

"For your info, Mercedes is out of town."

"Well, in that case, I'll be right over. What's the address?"

"555 Savannah Dr.; and hurry up."

"I'm on my way."

I hung up the phone, grabbed my shower bag, and headed for the bathroom. After taking a quick shower, I got dressed.

I had some unfinished business to tend to, and I was determined to finish it today.

## McKenzie

I was looking through some rough drafts of a new project I would start next month when Sylvia's voice came over the intercom.

"Mr. Taylor, Mr. Everette, is here to see you."

"Thanks, Sylvia, I'll be right there."

It seems like I've been waiting forever for this information. I motioned for Harold to come in.

"Hello Harold, how are you?" I said, closing the door behind him.

"I'm fine. How are you?"

"I'm anxious to find out what you found."

"Well, I won't keep you in suspense, let's get started."

"Good."

"McKenzie, before I give you this information, I want to ask you, are you sure you want to know?"

I looked at him like he was crazy. "Yes, why wouldn't I want to know? Stop stalling and give it to me."

"I just like to ask all my clients that question to give them one last chance to change their minds."

"Well, have any of them ever changed their minds?

"Just one," Harold chuckled. "No matter what kind of hardship it brought, they all wanted to know."

"Okay, well, so do I."

Harold handed me the envelope.

"In this envelop are photos and documentation of everything I observed in the past month on Mrs. Taylor's activities."

I opened the envelope. First, there was a picture of Sharon kissing a man in front of a restaurant. It was Lenny's Seafood & Bar, but I couldn't see his face. The next picture I saw, I just sat there staring; mouth open, but no words.

Harold watched me but said nothing. Finally, he cleared his throat and asked if I had any questions.

I still couldn't speak. I sat back in my chair, focused on the pictures that were on the desk in front of me.

"Are you alright?"

"No, Harold, I'm not alright. Is this everything?"

"Yes."

"Thank you. That will be all for now. I need to digest all of this."

"I understand. If you have any questions, give me a call. I will see my way out," He made his way over to the door. He glanced back at me. "I was hoping I didn't find anything."

"Yeah, me, too."

After Harold left, I sent Sylvia home for the day, so I wouldn't have any more interruptions while I read all of the information.

I picked up the stack of papers that I had laid aside out of the envelope. I flipped through the first couple of pages. They were all about our agreement and disclosure. Then there it was.

### *Monday: January 13, 2009 10:00am*

Mrs. Taylor left the resident at 10:00 am. At (10:45 am), She pulled into the driveway of 2855 Battlefield Ave., a brick home.

While waiting, I had my assistant check the owner of the resident.

Home is owned and occupied by Byron Jefferson, CEO of Princeton Enterprises.

Mrs. Taylor was at this resident until 3:00 pm. When she left, Mr. Jefferson walked her to the car, and they shared a passionate kiss before she got into her car and left. (Photo attached with date and time)

Mrs. Taylor then drove to Winnie food mart, bought a few items, and proceeded to go home. She arrived back at 4:00 pm, where she stayed for the rest of the night.

***Ended surveillance at 10:00 pm***

### *Tuesday: January 14, 2009 11:00am*

Mrs. Taylor left the resident at 11:00 am. She drove to the park on the south end of town, where Byron Jefferson was waiting for her.

At 11:25 am, she got into his vehicle, and he proceeded to drive.

At 11:50 am, they arrived at the Hyatt hotel. Once inside, they continued to the elevators. I was able to join them on the elevators, pretending I too was staying at the hotel.

Mr. Jefferson selected the 24th floor. I told him I was also staying on that floor.

While in the elevator; He and Mrs. Taylor began kissing and rubbing all over each other.

Once off the elevator, they walked to room 2401 and stopped. I quickly walked, passed them, and snapped a picture with my hidden camera. (Photo attached with date and time)

2:00 pm room service delivered meals to the room.

3:30 pm, they left the hotel, where he drove back to the park, and Mrs. Taylor got into her vehicle and left; again, sharing a passionate kiss with Mr. Jefferson before leaving. (Photo attached)

4:10 pm she arrived home and didn't leave anymore that day.

***surveillance ended at 10:00 pm***


I read every page of Harold's documentation. Each page felt like a knife pierced me in my heart, but nothing prepared me for what I would learn about my wife in the last few pages of the documents.

I couldn't believe after all we've been through, Sharon would do this to me. It's over.

If Byron is who she wants, then she can have him. They deserve each other.

I walked over to the bar and poured a double shot of crown and swallowed it in one big gulp - no chaser; no ice. The liquid burned my throat as it went down. I didn't care. There was nothing that could beat the pain I was feeling. I poured another shot and did the same.

I sat down at my desk, staring at the photos. I was hurt and angry, as hate slowly invaded my heart.

## Mercedes

At 11:30 am, a black Mercedes pulled into my yard. I tried to see who it was but couldn't because the tint on the windows was too dark and the car parked in the garage.

About thirty minutes of waiting, I decided to walk around the back of the house to see what was going on.

As I began to put my key in the door, I could hear moaning from inside. I know he's not doing what I think he's doing.

I opened the door and received the shock of my life. My entire world came crumbling down. There Richard was bent over the kitchen table while another man was banging him.

"What the hell is this?" They both jumped. "Oh My God, Richard, you're gay!"

"Mu- Mercedes wait a minute, it's not what you think."

"What do you mean it's not what I think. You're having sex with another man!" I started to feel nauseous. "Oh My God, I can't believe this! The man was scrambling to get his clothes on, while Richard stood there naked, trying to plead his case.

"Babe, let me explain."

"Let you explain? What is there to explain Richard? You need to get your things and get out of my house!" I grabbed a knife off of the counter.

"Mercedes, okay, pu -put the knife down. We're leaving." He held his hands up.

"Richard, I'm going to leave before I hurt you. When I get back, you need to have all your shit out of my house, and I mean, don't you leave a damn thing behind. Leave the key to my house on the counter. Do I make myself clear?" Not waiting for an answer. I threw the knife in the sink and walked out of the door.

I ran to my rental car, got in, and started driving. I didn't know where I was going, but I had to get away quickly.

One hour later, I pulled into the parking lot of McKenzie's office. Great, he's still here. I tried to open the door, but it was locked, so I banged on the door, hoping he was there.

When he opened the door, he looked a mess. His clothes were tattered, and I could smell  alcohol on his breath. At that moment, he made me forget about my problem.

"McKenzie, what happened?"

"Come on in, Mercedes."

He turned around, and I stopped to pick up a yellow envelope someone had slid under his door. I followed him to his office. He gestured for me to take a seat.

"What brings you here?"

"I need someone to talk to, but you look like you can use an ear, too." He smiled a weak smile.

"Yeah, I guess I can, but you go first."

"Man, you won't believe what just happened to me."

"With the day I've had nothing surprises me." He said, sitting down at his desk. "So, what happened?"

I told him all about the events of my day.

McKenzie had this look of shock on his face. "I told you, you wouldn't believe it."

"Damn, my boy went out like that?"

"You damn right, he did."

We chatted a little more about my situation, and then I asked him.

"So, what's going on with you?"

He handed me a stack of papers on his desk.

"Have fun."

"What is this?" I asked

"Just read it. It's all there."

"Okay. By the way, this was on your floor." I handed him the envelope.

He looked at it. "There's no returned address on it," he said curiously.

While I was reading the papers he had given me. he opened the envelope.

I couldn't believe Sharon did him like this. He doesn't deserve this. I looked up at him, and he was standing there, staring at the photos from the envelope.

"What?" I asked.

He got up and poured himself a drink, throwing the pictures down on his desk.

"Take a look for yourself."

I stood and took the pictures off his desk.

"You got to be kidding me!"

"What!"

"Richard and Sharon are seeing the same guy!"

"This is the guy I caught Richard with inside my house."

"Well, this just gets better and better."

"All of this is just too much for me to handle." I  sat back down and started crying.

McKenzie poured me a drink and sat next to me on the couch. He handed me the glass and placed his arm around my shoulders.

"Mercedes, it's going to be okay."

"How could they do this to us?"

"I don't have an answer to that, but I know I will be speaking with a divorce lawyer in the morning because there is no way in hell I'm going to continue to stay in this marriage."

"I told Richard to get his things out of my house, and don't leave anything there."

"Mercedes."

"Yeah," I said, still in my thoughts.

"Did you read the part where Sharon got rid of my babies?"

"She did what!"

"Yep, she got rid of my babies. She used a fake name, but her correct social security number, so when the PI I hired ran her through his database, all of it came back." McKenzie started crying. "How could she kill my babies? Why would she do that? They were innocent in all of this." He sobbed.

"McKenzie, I'm so sorry."

After he gained his composure, he stood.

"Hey, you want another drink?"

"Yes, and make it a double."

He poured our drinks, and we continued talking about everything that happened. We ordered pizza and had it delivered; both of us were too drunk to drive by that time.

"Mmm, this pizza is so good," I said after taking a bite of the cheesy pepperoni pizza.

"Yeah, it is. Pizzaroma always has good pizza."

"This is my first time eating from there, but it won't be my last. This is so delicious."

He watched as I took another bite.

"Why are you looking at me like that?" I asked.

"You are so beautiful."

"Thank you."

"You have some sauce on the side of your mouth."

"Oh, will you hand me a napkin, please?"

Instead of giving me a napkin, he leaned over and licked the sauce off the side of my mouth. I honestly didn't know how to respond to that. My mind was saying no, but my body failed me. My bud started to throb.

He studied my face, then leaned in to kiss me.

"Mercedes, what are we doing? He mumbled between breaths.

"I don't know, but I don't want to stop."

"Neither do I."

He unbuttoned my shirt and began kissing my neck, slowly going down to my chest. He unhooked my bra with one swift movement. He looked down at my breast, then back up at me.

"You're so beautiful," he said, just before taking one of my erect nipples into his mouth. I let out a moan.

This man was running me crazy. He sucked one breast and then the other, lightly teasing each nipple between his teeth.

"Oh McKenzie, what are you doing to me?" I gasped in pleasure.

"This is just the beginning."

He unfastened my pants. I lifted my butt so he could pull them down. He had a look of desire in his eyes that sent chills up my spine. He was turning me on big time.

He began kissing my stomach, leaving a trail of small kisses from my naval down to my flower. He teased my bud with his warm mouth, causing my arousal to intensify.

My head was spinning, rays of pleasure shooting through my body, causing me to tingle all over. When I reached the peak of ecstasy, my body began to jerk, and he entered me slowly, filling my inner hole. I moved my hips to match his rhythm as he glided in and out of me. I wrapped my legs around his waist. He began moving faster and faster, with each stroke deeper than the last, causing the fire that radiated through our bodies to intensify until finally, we reached our climax. He held me in his arms as we both lay there, trying to catch our breath.

"That was wonderful," I said.

"That was better than wonderful. I haven't had it that intense in a long time."

I sat up in panic mode, and looked at McKenzie.

"Mercedes, what's wrong?"

"We didn't use any protection."

"I know." He pulled me back down into his arms.

"But what if I end up pregnant?"

"Then, I will be there for you."

"You know there is a lot we need to consider."

"Yeah, I know. I am fully aware of all that, but right now, I want to enjoy this moment, besides, if either one of us has anything, there's a possibility we both have it since the two of them are screwing the same guy."

## Richard

After Byron left, I packed all of my things. Before leaving, I sat down at the kitchen table and wrote Mercedes a long letter; apologizing for the way I treated her. She didn't deserve any of it, and I hope one day, she would be able to forgive me. I left the letter on the counter, along with the key, and headed to Geri's.

The bar wasn't busy at all, so I opted to sit at a table in the far corner of the room. I ordered two double shots of cognac and swallowed them both down, back to back. I waved the waitress down and ordered two more of the same. I thought about all the things that have happened to me in my past and my present. Life just has not been fair; everything I've loved, I've lost, beginning with my childhood.

My mother, Vivian Madison, was a crack head. She was twenty-three when she had me. The night I was born, she was on crack. According to my grandmother. child protective services took me right out of her arms.

My grandparents, Momma Lee and Papa George raised me. Yeah, I'm a good old country boy from Birmingham, Alabama.

Life was great until I was twelve years old. My grandfather died of a heart attack. I remember it like yesterday. Papa George loved to watch western movies on Sunday evenings, and I enjoyed watching them with him. So, there we were sitting in the living room watching a western movie, while Momma Lee cooked dinner. It was raining, and I mean, it was raining hard.

I noticed Papa George sweating and holding his chest. When I asked him if he was okay, he said he was fine and that he just had a little heartburn. During the commercial break, papa stood up and told me he was going to the bathroom, but he never made it. He dropped dead right at my feet.

I remember hearing my grandmother screaming, crying, begging him not to leave us. I'm unsure when the ambulance arrived because I was in shock, unable to speak or move. I couldn't believe it, just like that he was gone.

My mother showed up for the funeral. I was surprised because she hadn't been by in a year. We didn't know if she was dead or alive. She looked good, though. She told us she had gotten off drugs and was working. She wanted me to come live with her. She and my grandmother talked privately about it. They agreed that I should go with her. I didn't protest, because I thought it would be great living with my mom. That's all I wanted for a very long time. But boy, was I wrong.

My mom was living with a man named Leo. At first, he seemed nice, but after being there a month, I overheard him beating my mom one night, saying to her that she was going to pay for smoking up his shit. I didn't know how he was going to make her pay, but I soon found out.

He called me into the living room where they were.

"Ray, Ray," he said, calling me by my nickname. "Your momma here has been a bad girl. She's done smoked up my shit. Now somebody got to pay."

I looked at my momma. She was sitting in a chair crying. Her hands were tied behind her back, and her face was severely beaten. Fear came over me as I stood there, afraid to speak.

"You and I are gone play a lil game, and your momma here gon watch," he said, grabbing me.

My heart was racing. I tried to snatch myself out of his grip, but I couldn't.

"Let me go!" I screamed.

"I will when I'm finished, witcha."

I started biting and hitting him. Of course, that really made him mad. He punched me in the face so hard that it knocked me down to the floor.

"You better not move, or the next time, you gon have a dead momma," he threatened.

I didn't move. I could hear my momma begging him not to hurt me. He punched her in the face again and told her to shut up, or he would kill her.

He looked down at me.

"Turn over on your stomach."

I shook my head no, and by this time, I was crying hysterically, begging him not to hurt me and to let me go.

"Please," I said, shaking my head.

"You better do like I say, boy, or I'm a kill your momma." He pulled the gun from behind his back and pointed at me. "Hush that crying, boy." He forcefully turned me on my stomach and held me down. "You gon enjoy this."

He unfastened his pants, pulled down my pajamas, and in one quick thrust, he forced himself inside me. I screamed. I was in pain, so much pain. I prayed God would take my life so that I could leave my body. I lost my soul that night. Life as I knew it was over.

I could still see my mother crying, telling me how sorry she was as he raped me, with each thrust ripping my insides more and more. All the apologizing in the world couldn't replace the pain I endured that night.

"You got a nice piece of ass right there. Now, go clean yourself up," he said as he zipped his pants.

He untied my momma.

"Go cook me something to eat."

He kicked her down as she  walked to the kitchen. She cooked his meal and then came to check on me. I lay in the bed, crying. I wanted to die.

When she entered my room, I told her to get out. I hated her. I couldn't stand the sight of her. I left that house before the sun came up that morning, and have never seen my mother again until I was looking down at her lifeless body in a casket.

When I left my mother's house, I went to the streets. One night, while I was looking through a dumpster for food. I met this lady named "Gem." She was a prostitute. She let me stay with her, but I had to pay rent. She introduced me to her pimp, and like her, I too became his property. Life, for me, was hard. Some of the tricks didn't want to pay, and there were times I was beaten.

When I turned fourteen, one of my johns almost killed me. I was stabbed five times in an alley and left to die. One of the city workers collecting trash found me and called an ambulance. I was barely breathing.

While lying in the hospital bed, I realized two things. I was blessed to be alive, and I had to get out of that situation. After I was released from the hospital, I caught the next thing smoking back to Birmingham.

My grandmother picked me up from the bus station. Boy, did it feel good to have her wrap her arms around me and tell me she loved me. She asked me where I had been; said my mom had called her a couple of times wanting to know if I was with her. I told her I didn't want to talk about it, and she dropped the subject. I think deep down inside, she knew what had happened, but we never talked about it.

Three months after, I returned to Birmingham, my grandmother received a call from the authorities in Mississippi, telling us my momma  died of an overdose of heroin. I couldn't cry. Even looking at her in that casket, I didn't cry. I wasn't sad, but angry. It was her drug addiction that ended her life and destroyed mine.

I hooked up with some guys in the

neighborhood. They called themselves the "Extremes." I started making that fast money. It was all good until I got shot at age seventeen by one of our rival's "Big Lu."

That was the pivoting point in my life. I decided I was going to get a real job, and that's just what I did.

I got a job at Main Crafts where they made parts for cars. The pay was decent but not as good as the money I made on the streets. However, I was trying not to go back down that road again.

One day, while I was at work, a couple of my co-workers invited me out to a strip club. I gladly took them up on the offer. That was my first time going, and I was excited. It was wild. Men were putting money in the ladies' G-strings. I couldn't believe how much money those ladies would walk off the stage with. It was insane, and they didn't have to prostitute themselves to make it.

After that night, I would sit and fantasize about being on that stage. I could see myself swinging on that stripper pole, having men and women putting their money in my G-string.

The next time I went back to the club, a tall, dark, and handsome gentleman asked could he sit at my table. I told him yes, and he sat down. He told me his name was Drew, He was an older man but had the body of a bouncer, and he wasn't that bad on the eyes either.

We hit it off that night in more ways than one. He invited me to Club Gemini the following weekend. When I got there, he introduced me to Donte, and after a few appearances there, I finally got the nerve to ask Donte one night if I could work in his club as a stripper. He said yes, and the rest is history. A performer was born that night.

I finished my drink and decided to go to Byron's. I called him, but he didn't answer. So, I got into my car and drove there anyway. When I got to his house, Sharon's car was parked in the driveway. What the hell is she doing here? I wondered as I parked my car next to hers.

**Sharon**

When I woke up this morning, McKenzie had already left, thank goodness. I didn't want to get into an argument with him. It seems as though that is all we do lately.

I called Grace Salon & Spa and made an appointment for one o'clock this afternoon. I wanted to get a complete makeover, which included getting my hair done, a facial, manicure, pedicure, and full body massage.

I'm going to surprise Byron tonight with dinner, and later, he can have me for dessert.

I thought about calling McKenzie but decided against it. I didn't need him ruining my mood, so I opted to go for a morning run.

When I returned home, I took a shower and got dressed. I made myself a strawberry-banana smoothie and headed to my appointment. Grace Salon & Spa was a thirty-minute drive from my house, but I didn't mind the ride, because it was all worth it in the end. Grace 's was the best in town.

After my massage, I went to the mall to pick up some sexy lingerie for my night with Byron. I made a quick stop at the grocery store to pick up items for dinner. I decided to make grilled salmon, wild rice, sautéed vegetables, green salad, and dinner rolls. I grabbed a bottle of red wine to go with the meal.

When I got to Byron's house, he wasn't home, so I grabbed the spare key from the secret hiding place in his garage and let myself in. Once I got all of the groceries in the house, I called him.

"Hello," he answered, in his sexy voice.

"Hey babe, what are you doing?"

"I'm at the office right now, working on some things."

"Well, how long will you be?"

"I don't know, a couple of hours or so?"

"I need to talk to you. Call me when you're on your way home."

"You sure?"

"Yes, it can wait. I'll talk to you later."

"Okay."

"Bye."

"Bye."

I hung up the phone. That gives me plenty of time to take a bubble bath and relax before starting dinner.

I finished putting up the groceries and ran my bath. Mmm, how I love the scent of lavender and vanilla. Before sitting down in the water, I turned on the radio system in the shower wall. Soft jazz played through the speakers. I sat down in the hot bathwater, and before I knew it, I had fallen asleep. I don't know how long I was sleeping, but when I opened my eyes, I was startled by Byron standing in the doorway.

"Hello, Angel," he said with a big grin on his face.

"Whew, you scared me." I clenched my chest.

"I'm sorry. You looked so beautiful lying there, I just wanted to take it all in."

"Aww, you always say the sweetest things," I smiled.

"Do you want some company?"

"Of course," I nodded.

He undressed and sat behind me in the bath, cradling his arms around me. He began kissing my neck while gently massaging my nipples. My center began to ache. He put one of his hands between my legs and began to tease my bud. I could feel his hardness in the lower part of my back. I turned my head to kiss him. He penetrated my flower with his finger and began sliding it in and out. He added a second finger, and I began to moan as the heat started to build up in the pit of my stomach. I gyrated against his fingers as he massaged my bud. My body began to shake uncontrollably. The sound of my scream was muffled from his kiss.

Facing him, I lowered myself on his thickness and began to ride him. He grabbed my butt and started moving my hips to match his thrusts. The faster he went, the wetter I got.

I tightened my grip around his hardness. His body began to jerk, and he exploded inside of me. I wrapped my arms around his neck, and we shared a soft intimate kiss.

"Hey, let's shower and get out of here," he suggested.

"Well, I was going to surprise you by cooking dinner, but I fell asleep, and the rest is history," I smiled at him as we continued to get dress.

"How about we cook dinner together?" He pulled me into his arms and kissed me.

I stepped out of his embrace and headed for the kitchen. "Come on before we never make it out of this bedroom."

While we prepared dinner, Byron grabbed two wine glasses and poured us each a glass of wine.

"Babe, everything smells so good."

"Thank you, and I must say you are a great helper in the kitchen."

"Girl, I don't know what you're talking about. I'm a master in the kitchen."

We both laughed.

"Hey, what is it you wanted to talk to me about?" He asked, as he sliced the tomatoes for the salad.

"Nothing. I just wanted to know what time you would be getting home so I could surprise you with dinner. I was trying to throw you off."

He picked me up and sat me on the countertop and began kissing me. He lifted my shirt over my head and cupped one of my breasts.

The doorbell chimed. He groaned and helped me put my shirt back on before going to answer it. I jumped down from the counter and ran my fingers through my hair to make sure I was presentable.

I turned the dial on the stove to low, so the food wouldn't burn and headed down the hall to see who Byron was talking to in the den. As I got closer, I stopped in the hallway and eavesdropped.

"You are going to have to leave," Byron told the guy.

"I'm not going anywhere. You can tell her to leave."

I peeped into the den and quickly recognized it was Richard. I decided to listen a little more before walking into the room.

"You have to give me some time. I haven't told her yet." Byron said.

"Oh well, I suggest you get to it because I'm not leaving."

"Look, give me a couple of hours and come back. I promise you, I will tell her everything."

"Hell to the no! Where she at? She shouldn't be here anyway." He pushed his way past Byron. "I will tell her myself."

"Don't do this."

Byron grabbed Richard's arm, and Richard snatched away from him.

"Okay, I tried to be nice, but you don't want to cooperate. Get out of my house!"

"You want me out? He said, pointing to his chest. "Nah, you going to have to put me out."

"That can be arranged. Now, you can go peacefully, or I can make it hell for you."

"Oh, it's like that, huh. You weren't saying that this morning when you had me bent over that table."

"Get the hell out now!"

I grabbed my chest. It felt like someone had just kicked me in it. I stepped into the den.

"What did you say?" I asked.

"You heard me!" Richard yelled.

"Byron, is this true?"

"Hell yeah, it's true," Richard interrupted.

"Shut up, Richard. I'm talking to Byron."

"Tell her, Byron!"

"Sharon, it's not like that," Byron said.

"Well, how is it then?" I asked.

Richard stood there with a smirk on his face, hands across his chest, tapping his foot. Byron didn't say anything.

"You better start talking," I said, getting angrier by the minute.

"Yeah, start talking, Byron," Richard mocked.

Byron rubbed his hands over his face and sighed heavily.

"Sharon, we can talk about this after Richard leaves."

"Oh no, there's no talking after Richard leaves. How long have you two been seeing each other?" Not waiting for an answer, I asked. "Does Renae know about this, Byron?"

"Honey, I am Renae!" Richard blurted out, with his hands on his hips, wringing his neck, like a sister with an attitude.

"What do you mean, your Renae?"

"Just, what I said!" He snapped.

"Oh my God! Does Mercedes know?"

"Oh yeah, she knows. She caught us this morning. Isn't that right, Byron?"

Now, I was crying and full of rage.

I reached for the iron candle holder on the table and began swinging it.

I hit Richard on the arm and back. Byron lunged at me, and I hit him in the face. His mouth started to bleed. Richard grabbed me from behind.

"Let me go, Richard."

"I can't do that until you calm down."

"Sharon babe, I'm so sorry. I didn't mean for things to happen this way," Byron said.

"Bullshit, everything you did was intentional. Now, you have jeopardized my life. I started crying hysterically and slid to the floor. "I risked everything for you, Byron."

## McKenzie

After Mercedes left my office, I waited until I sobered up a little before heading home. When I got there, I was not surprised to see that Sharon wasn't there. Actually, I was glad she wasn't. I needed to shower and get my thoughts together before seeing her.

"Hey, you," Mercedes answered in a low voice. "I wasn't expecting to hear from you until tomorrow."

"Yeah, still have a lot on my mind. When I got home, Sharon wasn't here, and she hasn't made it home, so it's giving me time to think."

"Where do you think she is?"

"You know where she is. Better yet, you know who she's with. She's going to have to go."

"Are you going to tell her about us?"

"No, I'm not. It's none of her business what I do or who I see anymore. After receiving the information I received today, the two of us are over. I don't care to be in the same room with her, let alone in a marriage."

Mercedes shifted the conversation.

"McKenzie, I want to thank you for being there for me today."

"Oh, so we are going back to being formal now, huh? Like what happened between us today never happened?"

"I didn't mean it that way. I was just saying thanks."

"Mercedes, let me say this to you. What you and I shared today meant something to me, and I don't want it to end as fast as it began. I want to explore the possibilities of what we started, and I hope you feel the same way."

"McKenzie, you know this puts me in a difficult situation. Sharon is my best friend."

That was not the response I was looking for. I was hoping she would give us a try.

"I tell you what. I'll give you a few days to think about it. I'll talk to you later." I said, hanging up the phone.

**Sharon**

Sirens, red, and blue lights flashing. It was like something out of a movie scene. My head was pounding, and I felt dizzy. My heart was racing, and my clothes were covered in blood.

There is a cop standing next to the patrol car. His mouth was moving, but I couldn't understand what he was saying.

"Will someone tell me what's going on here?" I started screaming. I tried to get out of the car, but I was in handcuffs. I kicked the door, and the officer that was standing by the vehicle walked over to me.

"Ma'am, please don't do that."

"Officer, what is going on?" He looked at me as if I was some alien from another planet.

"What the hell is going on?" I screamed.

Still, he said nothing. I watched as he walked away. He stopped to talk to Richard, who was also covered in blood. I looked for Byron, but I didn't see him. *What the hell is going on?* I saw an ambulance speed off with red lights and siren. The officer walked back to the car.

"Sharon Taylor, you are under arrest."

"Under arrest, for what?"

"You have a right to remain silent. Anything you say can and will be used against you in a court law."

"What did I do?" I yelled!

"You have the right to speak to an attorney. If you cannot afford an attorney, one will be appointed to you."

"I didn't do anything," I scream.

"Do you understand these rights as they have been read to you?"

"Officer, will you please tell me what I am being arrested for, please!"

"Aggravated assault with a deadly weapon."

"Aggravated assault with a deadly weapon?" I repeated, bewildered.

"Ms. Taylor, do you understand the rights I just read to you?"

"Yes." I started to cry. "Officer, will you call someone for me?"

"When you get to the jail, you will be allowed to make a phone call."

At the jail, I sat in a room with gray walls. It was so depressing. The only furniture in it was a table with two chairs, placed on opposite sides of it, and one light fixture that hung over it. The room had the smell of new paint.

I have seen enough crime shows to know what would happen next. So, I sat quietly and waited for the investigator.

I was drifting off to sleep when the door opened. I looked up and saw a short, bald, white guy, dressed in a shirt and tie. I knew he was the investigator, and following him was the officer that arrested me.

The investigator sat down across from me. He extended his hand to initiate a handshake, while the officer stood by the door.

"Hello, Ms. Taylor. I'm Investigator Millings. How are you?"

*How the hell do you think I am!* "Hello."

He cleared his throat. "Ms. Taylor, can you tell me what happened tonight?"

"I don't know what happened. I've been asking that question all night, and no one has answered me yet."

The investigator sat back in his chair and stared at me.

"Ms. Taylor."

"It's Mrs. Taylor."

"Excuse me, Mrs. Taylor, are you trying to tell me you do not remember stabbing Byron Jefferson?"

"Hold up! You think I stabbed Byron?"

I was shocked and confused.

"Not think; we know you did."

"I didn't stab Byron. I couldn't have stabbed him."

"And why is that, Mrs. Taylor?"

"Because I love him, and I wouldn't hurt him, that's why!"

"Do you know how many times we have heard that?"

I sat there, shaking my head as tears rolled down my face.

"Is he alright?"

"He's in bad shape. Now, are you ready to talk, Mrs. Taylor?"

## Mercedes

Awakened out of my sleep, I rolled over to look at my alarm clock. Who in the world could be calling me at two o'clock in the morning?

"Hello."

"Hello Mercedes. This is Sharon. I need a favor," she said through tears.

"Sharon, what's wrong?" I sat up in bed.

"I'm in jail."

"You're in jail, for what?"

"They got me for aggravated assault with a deadly weapon. That charge can change to murder depending on the outcome of the victim's condition."

"What! What happened?"

"I don't know. The investigator said I stabbed someone, but I didn't do it."

"Who is the person, Sharon?" I asked since it was apparent, she wasn't going to give me that detail.

"It's Byron Jefferson, Mercedes. He's in bad shape." She sobbed.

"Does McKenzie know about this?"

"No, and don't tell him. I don't want him to find out."

"Sharon, just how do you think you're going to keep this a secret? It's going to be all over the news in the morning."

"I didn't think about that. I don't know what to do."

"Times up," The guard said, in the background.

"Mercedes, I'll go before the judge tomorrow. I'll call you okay."

"Hey, wait, what time tomorrow?"

"Nine o'clock in the morning," she said, before hanging up.

I sat in my bed, not believing what I had just heard. I quickly dialed McKenzie's number.

"Hello."

*His sleepy voice even sounds sexy.* "McKenzie, it's Mercedes. I have something to tell you about Sharon."

"I don't want to talk about Sharon. It's almost three in the morning for goodness sake."

"This is very important. Sharon just called me and told me she's in jail."

"She's in jail, what for?"

*Now, he's awake.* "Yes, she said she's charged with aggravated assault with a deadly weapon.

"Say that again."

"Aggravated assault with a deadly weapon," I repeated.

"Did she say what happen?"

"Yeah, she said, she's accused of stabbing someone."

"Did she tell you who?"

"Yes, its Byron," I said in a low voice.

"Byron!" His voice rang loud through the line. "Mercedes, thanks for calling me. I'm about to head down to the police station to see what's going on."

"McKenzie, I don't think that's a good idea."

"Why?"

"She told me not to tell you."

There was nothing but silence on the line.

"McKenzie, are you there?"

"Good night, Mercedes."

I jumped out of bed and got dressed. I was going to meet McKenzie at the jail, although he didn't know I was coming.

When I pulled in the parking lot, McKenzie was walking inside of the police station. I honked the horn, but he didn't turn around. I hurried and parked the car and ran into the station to try and catch up with him.

"Hey," I said almost out of breath.

"What are you doing here?"

"I came for support."

He didn't say anything. He looked back at the officer, who stood there, observing the both of us.

"Officer, is there any way I could speak to my wife?"

He shook his head. "I'm sorry, sir, not tonight. Visitation is tomorrow morning at ten."

"Well, can I speak with the arresting officer?"

"Sure, have a seat. He's out on patrol, but I can have him come to the station."

"Thank you," McKenzie said as we took our seats.

## McKenzie

When Mercedes called and told me Sharon was in jail, I didn't know what to think.

I came down to the police station to speak with her because I wanted some answers, but they won't let me see her. Good thing, though, because I may have ended up behind bars myself.

Mercedes touched my thigh, and that brought me out of my train of thought.

"It's going to be okay."

I sighed, "No, it isn't."

I looked up just as the officer walked through the door.

"Mr. Taylor?"

"Yes."

"Hello sir. I'm Officer Bradley, how can I help you?"

"I would like to know what is going on with my wife."

"Right now, all I can tell you is that she is being charged with the stabbing of Mr. Byron Jefferson. He is in critical condition and its touch and go."

"I don't believe my wife would do something like that. What did she say?"

"She said she doesn't remember doing it, but there was a witness on scene."

"A witness, who is it?"

"I'm afraid I can't reveal that information right now because of the investigation. But you can call or come by in the morning and speak with Investigator Millings."

"I understand. Thanks for your time."

"You're welcome."

Mercedes and I walked back to our cars.

"You want to grab a cup of coffee?" I asked.

"You read my mind. Actually, I could eat a little something right now." She smiled.

"There's a Denny's down the street."

"Sounds good to me. I love their pancakes."

## Sharon

"Wake up, Sunshine," the jailer said, as she banged on the bars of the cell with her nightstick.

I sat up in the small cot that they call a bed.

"You have a visitor this morning."

I stood, and the guard unlocked the door. She instructed me to turn around. She placed handcuffs around my wrists and led me down the hall. Women were standing at the bars, watching me as I passed by. One of the ladies yelled, "What did you do?"

I wish I knew, I mumbled to myself.

After a couple of turns, we stopped in front of the interrogation room that I was in last night. The jailer unlocked the door and told me to have a seat. Fifteen minutes later, my lawyer, Dean Winston, walked in.

"Dean, I'm so happy to see you."

"Sharon, how are they treating you in here?"

"I want to go home." I burst into tears.

"I'm going to try my best to get you out of here, I promise." He handed me a handkerchief from his suit jacket.

"When can I leave?"

"First, I need to ask you some questions. You have to go before the Judge in two hours, and I need to prep you for that." He peered through his thin rim glasses that sat low on his nose.

"What do you remember about last night?"

"I remember Byron, Richard, and me in his living room talking."

"Who is Richard?"

"He's my best friend's boyfriend."

Dean wrote that down on the notepad he had in front of him.

"Okay, what were you talking about?"

"I overheard Richard and Byron yelling in the den while I was in the kitchen, so I went to see what all the yelling was about. When I walked in, Richard was telling Byron that he better tell me something, or he would tell me himself."

"What was it he wanted Byron to tell you?"

"That they were lovers."

It took Dean a moment to digest what I had just revealed to him.

"Okay, so then what happened?"

"Well, after Richard blurted out that they were lovers, I started yelling at Byron and saying to him, how could he do this to me. Then I asked him did Renae, who I thought was his girlfriend, know about him being gay."

"What did he say?"

"He didn't say anything because Richard blurted out that he was Renae."

"Wow, how did this make you feel?" Dean sat back in his chair, waiting for my response.

"It made me angry."

"So, what did you do?"

"I ran towards Byron-" I paused.

"And," he said, waiting on me to complete my thought.

"I don't remember."

"You don't remember." He arched his eyebrows.

"No, I don't remember. The next thing I knew was I was sitting in the back of a patrol car being told that I was under arrest for stabbing Byron.

"Okay, I think I have what I need right now. I will see you in court in an hour." He put the notepad in his briefcase and stood from the table. The guard let him out of the room and led me back to my cell. God, please get me out of this situation and let Byron be okay.

I arrived at the courtroom at 8:45 am. When I walked in, I locked eyes with McKenzie and held my head down. I was too ashamed to look at him. The officer that arrested me was sitting in a chair on the opposite side of the room. The bailiff stood by the Judge's bench, and three other officers stood on opposite sides, providing security.

The courtroom was large and filled with cherry wood furniture. nNavy blue carpet covered the floors, and the walls were decorated with pictures of past judges who previously served on the bench.

I sat on the right side of the courtroom with my back to McKenzie. I was thankful I didn't have to see his face the entire time.

"All rise! This is the case regarding the State versus Sharon Taylor. The Honorable Judge Larkin presiding," the bailiff said.

Judge Larkin entered the courtroom. "All may be seated," she said, before taking a seat. "This hearing is for Mrs. Sharon Taylor. Mrs. Taylor, you have been charged with aggravated assault with a deadly weapon, depending on the outcome of Mr. Jefferson's condition, these charges could change. Who will be representing Mrs. Taylor?"

"I am, your honor." Dean raised his hand.

"State your name for court records."

"I'm Dean Winston, criminal law attorney, representing Mrs. Sharon Taylor."

"Mr. Winston, how does your client plead?"

"Your honor, she pleads not guilty."

"Okay. Now, we will discuss the bond and conditions of bond. I will hear from the state first."

The state attorney stood up.

"Your honor, we are requesting that the offender not be released from jail at this time due to the nature of the crime. The said victim is still in the hospital on life support. We may have more charges against the offender, based on the medical condition of the victim in the future. Also, there's the possibility of flight risk."

"What does the defendant have to say in regard to this statement?" The judge asked.

"Your honor, we are requesting a bond be set for Mrs. Taylor. She has no failure to appear or prior convictions and has never been in trouble with the law. Therefore, we have no reason to believe she would be a flight risk," Dean responded.

"Judge, although she doesn't have any priors, she most definitely has the monetary means to flee if she wanted to. We cannot take that chance," the state attorney replied.

"I will be right back."

The Judge got up and went to her chambers. After about thirty minutes, she returned.

"After carefully considering the arguing statements and looking at the documentation of this crime, the bond is denied. Mrs. Taylor, your next court appearance will be an arraignment with Judge Phoenix on June 15, 2009, at 1:30 pm. All parties are dismissed." She tapped her gavel.

I turned and looked at McKenzie as the deputy led me out of the courtroom. I noticed Mercedes sitting next to him. Hmmm, I didn't notice her earlier. I was glad to see she did come to support me.

While I sat in a room at the courthouse waiting for a deputy to transport me back to the jail, Dean came to see me.

"Sharon, I'm sorry. I was really hoping the judge would show some mercy and give you a bond."

"Yeah, I was too. So, what's next?"

"Pray Byron wakes up out of his coma and tells us what happened before your arraignment."

I nodded. *Lord, Please let him wake up.*

"Where is Richard?" I asked.

"No one can find him."

"What do you mean, no one can find him?"

"It's as if he just disappeared." He shrugged.

"Talk to Mercedes. She will tell you where he is."

"I've already done that. She said she hasn't heard from Richard."

"So, I'm going to go down for something I didn't do?" I started crying.

"He is on the most wanted list, and they are looking for him. Hopefully, they will find him soon."

The deputy came into the room to get me.

"I'll visit you soon, alright?"

I nodded as the deputy escorted me out of the building into the patrol car.

## McKenzie

Another week went by before I went to see Sharon. She had been calling me, but I wouldn't answer the phone. She would leave messages, apologizing, and asking me to visit her. However, I figured I would wait until my divorce lawyer had drawn up the divorce papers so I could deliver them personally along with the documentation from the PI.

After signing in and going through the security clearance, I was finally face to face with Sharon.

"McKenzie, I'm glad you came," She said.

I didn't respond, so she continued.

"I want to apologize to you for all that has happened. I didn't mean to hurt you this way. You didn't deserve this. I know now that I took you for granted, and I didn't appreciate you or all the things you've done for me. Please forgive me," she sighed.

"Sharon, you hurt me. I loved you with all my being. All I wanted was to spend my life with you. I'm sorry, but I can't accept your apology. I will never be able to get passed the things you've done."

"Please McKenzie, I know we can work through this. It was just the one time that I cheated. I promise I will never cheat on you again."

"You don't get it. It's not just the cheating. It's the lying. You sit here as if cheating is all you've done. Where is the remorse for killing my babies, huh?"

The look on her face was priceless.

"Yeah, I know about the abortions, not once, but twice you killed my baby. I will never forgive you for that."

"McKenzie, let me explain." She reached out to touch my hand, but I drew it back off the table.

"There's nothing to explain, Sharon. I want a divorce." I handed her the divorce papers.

"Please don't do this. Let's talk about it."

"There's nothing left to say. I want you out of my life for good. Maybe Byron will live and give you another chance. By the way, he's screwing Richard."

I stood up from the table. "I'll have my lawyer come back and pick up the divorce papers. That envelope is for you to keep. I have my own copies." I handed her the yellow envelope I had waited on purpose to give her. Then I turned and walked away without looking back as she called my name.

## Sharon

"McKenzie, help me!" I was going underwater, and he was watching me drown. His eyes were cold as ice and his face emotionless, while I struggled to stay afloat. He walked away, and I went under. I couldn't breathe.

I wake up and look around, relieved it was just a dream. I lay there in the dark, thinking about my visit with McKenzie. It's been two weeks now, and I haven't heard from him. I told his lawyer last week that I was not signing the papers. I thought surely by now, McKenzie would have come back to see me.

I need to get out of here if I'm going to save my marriage.

I spoke with my lawyer; still, no changes in Byron's condition, and no update on Richard's whereabouts. I've been remembering bits and pieces of that night, but they are not clear.

When I was able to make a call, I called Mercedes.

"Hey, it's Sharon."

"I know. What's up?"

"Will you talk to McKenzie for me? I need to see him, and he's not answering my calls."

"I can see what I can do."

"Thanks, you're the best."

"No problem."

"So, how are things with you?"

"I've just been busy working."

"Yeah, I see. You've been too busy to visit your girl," I said disappointedly.

"Girl, you know I love you. I promise I will come to visit you soon."

She didn't sound too convincing.

"Well, I'm not going to hold you. I will be looking forward to that visit."

"I'll see you soon."

"Mercedes, wait!" I called out before she hung up. "Have you heard from Richard?"

"No, I haven't heard from him at all. His cell phone is no longer in service."

"Damn. Well, have you heard anything about Byron?"

"No. Last I heard he was still on life support."

"Okay, thanks. Bye."

"Bye, Sharon."

Dean wasn't lying to me after all.

I returned to my cell and pulled out the envelopes from under my mattress. I looked at all the photos of Byron and me, proof of my infidelity, countless documentation of our meeting spots, and my abortions. How in the hell did he find out about my abortions? I pondered. That was supposed to be confidential. I'm going to sue them when I get out of here for breach of confidentiality.

Weeks had gone by, and I still hadn't heard from McKenzie. I think it's time to face the fact that it's over. He wants nothing to do with me.

I was sitting on the bed with the divorce papers in my hand when the guard came to my cell.

"Get your things, and let's go."

"What? Where are we going?"

"You are getting out."

I stood there, looking in disbelief.

"Move it," she snapped.

I quickly grabbed all my belongings and followed the guard. She stopped at the ladies' restroom and handed me a bag with clothes in it.

"You need to change."

I nodded and went in to change my clothes. After changing, the guard proceeded to take me to a small room where Dean was waiting for me.

"Hi," he said.

The guard closed the door.

"Hi Dean, is it true, I'm being released?"

"Yes." He motioned for me to sit down. "Byron is awake-"

"He is! When did he wake up?" I interrupted.

He nodded his head and continued.

"He woke up this morning. Investigator Millings talked to him, and he told him everything that happened, specifically stating that you were not the one who stabbed him."

"Aw, thank God!" I let out a sigh of relief.

"So, what did he say happened?"

"The detective said Byron wants to talk to you and tell you himself what happened."

"Okay, well, can we go?"

"Yes, we can, as soon as they get done processing you out of here."

When we arrived at the hospital, Dean walked with me to Byron's room.

"I'm going to stop right here and give you two some privacy. Do you want me to wait for you?"

"No. I will catch a cab to the house."

"Okay. Come to my office tomorrow so we can complete the paperwork."

"I will, and Dean, thank you." I hugged him.

I walked in the room and Byron lay there looking at me.

"Hello, beautiful."

"Hello, Byron, I'm so happy you are awake." I sat in the chair next to his bed.

He smiled. "I'm sorry, Sharon, for putting you through all of this."

"We can't change the past. What I want to know is what happened that night?"

"After you hit me with the iron candleholder, Richard grabbed you. You tried getting away from his grasp, but you couldn't, so you started crying. The smoke alarm went off, so I ran to the kitchen to turn off the food. By the time I got to the kitchen, Richard was right behind me. We started arguing again about the whole situation. When you walked in, he had just slapped me, and we started fighting. When I pushed him, he stumbled into you. I threw a punch at him; he ducked, and I punched you instead. When you fell to the floor, you must have hit your head pretty hard, because you didn't move. You were unconscious. I stopped to check on you, and when I did, Richard grabbed the knife off the counter and stabbed me in my back. When I turned around to stop him, he stabbed me again twice in my chest. According to the doctors, just inches from my heart."

"Who called the police?" I asked, trying to make sense of it all.

"Richard called the police and told them I was his friend, and he came by to visit me. When he didn't get an answer at the door, he used my spare key to come inside, and he found us like that. By the time they got there, I had lost a lot of blood and was unconscious, too."

"So, he made it look like I stabbed you."

"Yes."

"Have they found him?"

"No," he said sadly.

"It's going on two months now. He could be anywhere."

"How have you been?" Byron asked, changing the subject.

"Let's see. I have spent almost two months in jail since this ordeal. My marriage is over as far as McKenzie is concerned. He has made it clear he doesn't want anything to do with me and has filed for divorce. Hey, everything is just peachy!" I said, sarcastically.

"Sharon, I'm so sorry. If you need a place to stay, you can stay with me until you get a place of your own."

I gave him that 'I don't think so look.'

"No strings attached. I just want to help you. Besides, I'm not there anyway," he smiled.

"I'll keep that in mind, but I need to speak with McKenzie. We need to talk about everything that has happened."

"Does he know you're out?"

"No. McKenzie hasn't been answering the phone, so I didn't bother to call him and let him know. He'll know when I get home."

"Well, you know where the spare key is. You're welcome to stay if you need to."

"Thanks."

## McKenzie

"It's been great having you here."

"Just great, huh." Mercedes cocked her head and pursed her lips.

"Correction. It's been wonderful having you here." I pulled her into my arms.

"Uh-huh, I got you," she teased.

Mercedes and I had been spending a lot of time together lately, and I must say it has been outstanding, despite all the drama.

I was hoping to have been divorced by now. I didn't think Sharon would contest it, due to her infidelity and the proof thereof, but my lawyer told me she is refusing to sign the divorce papers. He's in the process of working on getting around that since she's in jail. So right now, it's a waiting game for me.

However, in the meantime, I am enjoying my time with Mercedes. Tonight, we are cooking dinner and watching a movie at my place.

"I'm going to check on the steaks," I said, walking out on the patio. "They are just about done."

"Good, because I'm starving."

When the food was ready, we decided to sit in the den and watch a movie while we eat.

"So, what movies did you pick up?" She asked.

"Oh, I grabbed an ole time favorite, "Friday.""

"Cool."

We ate and laughed during the entire movie.

After cleaning the kitchen, we poured ourselves a glass of wine and sat down to watch another movie, "All About the Benjamins."

An hour into the movie, Mercedes whispered in my ear. "Let's go upstairs." She stood and began walking towards the staircase. I turned off the television and followed her lead. Once in the bedroom, she lit a couple of candles and put a Marvin Gay disc in the CD player; "get up, get up, get up, get up…sexual healing, babe…" Mercedes was doing a striptease. I sat, mesmerized by her every move.

After she was completely naked, she started undressing me; first taking off my shirt, then my pants. She dropped to her knees and started teasing the top of my shaft. A moan escaped my lips. She continued this for several minutes. When she stood, I picked her up and laid her on the bed, flipping her on her stomach.

I planted small kisses down her spine. "Get on your knees," I said in a seductive whisper. I bent her over and found her budding flower.

"Oh, McKenzie," she moaned as I teased it with my tongue.

I grabbed her hips and entered her from behind.

"Ooh, you're so wet."

"You like that, daddy."

"Oh yeah. What the hell!".

## Sharon

I caught a cab from the hospital to Byron's house. A part of me was very disappointed to see my car still in his garage. Just another sign, McKenzie doesn't care anymore.

I got Byron's spare key and went inside the house. The stench from all of the rotten food overcame me, and I ran to the bathroom to throw up. I walked into the living room. There on the floor by the fireplace, was the iron candleholder and droplets of blood.

I walked in the kitchen and saw blood all over the place. There was rotten food on the stove; a reminder of how a perfect night resulted in a nightmare.

I couldn't let Byron come home to that. He'd been through so much already, so I spent all evening and part of the night cleaning the house. When I finished, I collected all of my things and headed home.

Arriving home, I noticed Mercedes' car was in our drive. I opened the door and heard music playing. I looked into the living room and saw two wine glasses. I went into the kitchen, and neither one of them were there. I looked out back on the patio; they weren't there either. My heart began to beat fast. I tiptoed up the stairs to listen carefully. The door was cracked, so I looked inside. Oh, Hell, No! In My Bed! I can't believe this shit!

I was furious. I went back downstairs into McKenzie's study and got his pistol out of his desk drawer. When I got back to the bedroom, I turned on the light switch. They both turned and looked at me.

"How could the both of you do this to me?" I said, pointing the gun at them.

Mercedes covered herself up with the covers, while McKenzie sprung up off the bed and held his hands up, trying to talk to me.

"Sharon, please, put the gun down."

"Shut up! How could you do this to me? And in our bed! McKenzie, what were you thinking?"

"Sharon, please put the gun down so we can talk." He moved slowly towards me, with his hands still in the air.

"Mercedes, how could you? I thought you were my friend, and you go behind my back and sleep with my husband!"

"I'm sorry, Sharon. It was a mistake," she said, crying. She was stood on the other side of the bed.

"Oh, this was no mistake. You knew what you were doing!"

"Forgive me, Sharon, please forgive me," she begged.

"How long have you two been seeing each other?"

"Babe, please put down the gun," he pleaded.

"Answer the question, McKenzie!"

"Not long, ba-a-be. J-Just after I found out about you and Byron."

He was now arm's length away from me.

"Don't come any closer."

He stopped. "Babe, let's start over."

"Oh, so now you want to start over."

He didn't say anything.

"Sharon, we can get passed this. We're sisters."

I aimed the gun at her and pulled the trigger.

McKenzie lunged at me. He tried to take the gun out of my hand, and I bit his arm. He grabbed me by my wrist, and the gun went off. He stopped and looked at me.

## McKenzie

"Sharon."

A look of panic covered her face as she stared at me, unable to talk. She looked down at her chest and dropped the gun. I picked her up and placed her on the bed.

I looked over at Mercedes, and she was groaning in pain. She'd been shot, too.

I got my cell phone off the nightstand and called 911.

"911, what's the location of your emergency?" The operator asked.

"25 Washington Place. Two people have been shot, hurry," I said, before ending the call.

"Mercedes, where are you shot?"

"I don't know. I feel pain all over," she cried.

"Okay. Calm down, babe, they are on their way."

I looked at Sharon. Her breathing was heavy.

"Sharon, hold on."

Suddenly, it hit me that Mercedes and I didn't have on any clothes. I got her dressed and then dressed myself, just in the nick of time, because the doorbell chimed.

I ran downstairs and opened the door. There were paramedics and police officers at the door.

"They are upstairs," I said, leading the way.

The paramedics started working on them right away. I heard one say that Sharon had lost a lot of blood, and her pulse was weak.

Mercedes was hit in the shoulder, and the bullet exited her back. She would be okay, but Sharon, they were not so sure of.

They put Sharon on a gurney and rushed her to the hospital, blaring lights and sirens, one of the patrol cars leading the way.

They placed Mercedes on a gurney and took her to the hospital in a second ambulance.

"Sir, can you tell me what happened?" The officer asked.

" Officer, can we do this later? My wife is in that ambulance, and they are not sure if she is going to make it. I need to get to the hospital." I said, crying and very distraught by this time.

"Sure, I will take you." He went over to another patrol officer and told him he was going to take me to the hospital.

When we got there, I got out of the car and ran into the E.R. The officer was right behind me. A lady was sitting at the check-in desk.

"The ambulance just brought my wife in, and I need to get back there to her."

"Sir, what's your wife's name?"

"Sharon Taylor."

"Hold on a minute. Let me go check."

I started pacing back and forth.

"Mr. Taylor, come sit down," the officer requested.

"I don't want to sit down. I want to see my wife."

Finally, the nurse returned.

"Mr. Taylor, you can come on back." She opened the doors and led the way, taking us to a small waiting room. "The doctor will be in to speak with you in a few minutes," she said before closing the door behind her.

The officer and I sat quietly. As a matter of fact, it was so quiet all you could hear was the ticking of the clock on the wall.

It seemed like forever before the doctor came in.

"Mr. Taylor."

"Yes."

"I'm Dr. Ingles. I'm sorry, sir, but Mrs. Taylor didn't survive her injuries."

"No!"

I placed my face in my hand.

"Is there anyone you would like for us to call for you?"

I shook my head, no.

"You can stay here as long as you like, Mr. Taylor. Let us know if you need anything," he said before he left.

While sitting there, an investigator from the Chicago PD come in.

"Mr. Taylor, I'm sorry for your loss."

"Thank you."

"Sir, we need to find out what happened back at your resident."

I nodded my head and proceeded to tell him everything that happened.

After he had finished getting the information, he left to talk to Mercedes, and I went to see Sharon.

When I walked into the hospital room, she looked as if she was asleep. Her skin was pale, and her tears had dried down her face. I wept.

"I never wanted this for us, Sharon. You were my world, the air that I breathed. All I ever wanted was to have a great life with you. I'm so sorry it ended this way. I love you."

I got myself together and walked out of the room. I went to the nurse's station.

"Can I help you, sir?"

"Yes, what room is Mercedes Wilkerson in?"

"She's in that room over there." She pointed. "The doctor is in the room with her right now."

"Thanks. If you don't mind me asking, how is she doing?" I wanted to prepare myself for the unknown.

"I'm not sure, but you can speak to her doctor once she comes out."

"Is it okay if I wait right here?"

"Sure, she should be out in a minute. Are you related to Ms. Wilkerson?"

"No. She's my wife's best friend. She doesn't have any family here."

"Oh, okay." She nodded.

When the doctor came out of the room, the lady called her over to us.

"Dr. Mathis, this is Mr. Taylor. He wants to know how Ms. Wilkerson is doing."

"She and the baby are doing fine?" She smiled.

"Baby," I repeated, now in shock.

"Yes. You can go see her if you like."

I shook my head, still processing the information.

When I opened her room door, she looked up at me and smiled. She had bandages wrapped around her shoulder and back.

"Hey, you," she smiled.

I went over to her bed. "A baby." I touched her belly.

"Yes, a baby."

She must have read the expression on my face.

She nodded. "Yes, it's yours. You're going to be a daddy."

Tears rolled down my face. And this time, they were tears of joy.

Mercedes was discharged from the hospital the following day. I stayed at her place to take care of her while she recovered and to have my home cleaned.

The investigation was concluded, and there were no charges filed. Sharon's death was ruled accidental.

On the day of her funeral, I was not prepared for the shock of my life.

During the funeral, there were many people there, along with family and friends, to pay their final respects. When it was time for the viewing, there was a young lady, last in line. She was dressed in all black with a veil covering her face. When she walked up to the casket, she just stood there as if she was paralyzed and couldn't move. I thought that was very odd. One of the ushers took her gently by the arm and escorted her back to her seat. While at the cemetery, I noticed her standing off a little bit, but when we all left, she stayed behind.

"Hmmm, I wonder who she is," I whispered to Mercedes.

"Me, too. Maybe she's one of her family members."

"Maybe," I shrugged.

The repast was at our home. Some family members and friends shared stories of Sharon and the time they spent together.

After everyone left, there was a knock at the door. When I opened it, there stood the beautiful young lady from the burial site. She was small built and had long wavy hair with caramel skin and a beautiful smile.

"Hello," I said.

"Hello, Mr. Taylor?" She asked.

"Yes."

"My name is Autumn Rivera. First, I would like to say I'm sorry for your loss."

"Thank you." I stepped out of the house onto the porch.

"I need to talk to you about your wife."

"What about her?"

"She's my mother."

"What did you say?"

"Sharon Taylor was my mother."

"Sweetheart, I'm sorry, but you must have the wrong Sharon Taylor. My wife never had any children."

"No, I have the right, Sharon. Here's a letter that my aunt gave me before she died a year ago."

I took the letter. "Come with me."

We entered the house and headed to the kitchen, where Mercedes was finishing up the dishes.

"Mercedes, this is Autumn, she says she's Sharon's daughter."

"What! There must be some mistake. Sharon and I were best friends. She never mentioned she had a daughter. As a matter of fact, she didn't want any children."

My heart sunk with that news.

"I know you have your doubts, but read the letter," Autumn insisted.

"Here, Mercedes, you read it." I handed her the letter. She took the note and inspected it.

"It was written a year ago," she said, confirming what Autumn had told us.

She began reading the letter.

*My Dearest Autumn,*

*Your Aunt Mattie wrote to me and told me she was very ill. She wanted you to know the truth about me, so here it is.*

*Your Dad and I were young and very much in love when we conceived you. I was thirteen, and he was sixteen. Our parents were very angry at us, but his parents accepted things for what they were, my parents, not so.*

*My father, your grandfather, wanted me to have an abortion, but your dad and I wanted you, so we ran away. The authorities found us and took us back home.*

*We all sat down and had a meeting to decide what was best for the three of us. Your dad and his family agreed to take care of you after you were born. During the first six months of your life, I would visit you every day.*

*Then one day, my dad comes home and tells us we were moving. We didn't just move out of state, but out of the country. He had gotten military orders to Germany. I didn't want to go because I didn't want to be away from you, but I was only thirteen and had nowhere else to go. I would write to your dad all the time and include a letter to you. Autumn, my heart was so broken. I pray you never experience that type of pain.*

*We were in Germany for about three months when I slipped into a depression. I saw countless doctors and counselors; they began medicating me to help me forget because I had become suicidal; I attempted to take my life twice.*

*We were there four years before relocating to California. You were still many miles away. I always felt deep down inside that he moved us to Germany to keep me away from you. When we got to California, it was confirmed. I overheard him telling my mom that we would never move back to Missouri as long as you and your dad were there.*

*Then, as fate would have it, my dad's brother died, and we went there for the funeral. I had my cousin Sherry take me to your grandparent's home. When we pulled up in front of their house, I saw you and your dad in the yard playing. I knew it was you because you looked just like me when I was your age. Your dad was swinging you around and around; oh, how you just laughed. The sound of your laughter just filled my heart.*

*Your dad and I locked eyes, and he put you down. You ran over to the picnic table, which I hadn't noticed before, and a woman was sitting there; she was pregnant. I noticed the wedding band on her finger, and when I looked back at your dad, I saw his wedding band also.*

*I told my cousin to drive. He had moved on with his life, and the two of you seemed happy. I didn't want to interfere with that, but I made a promise that day to myself that I would never have another child taken from me. So I never had any more children, and I never tried to contact him or anyone in his family.*

*When your aunt contacted me, she told me, your dad was killed while deployed in Iraq when you were nine years old, and that she and her husband raised you. She said when you were sixteen, she told you about me being your mother; and felt it was time for us to meet. I told her I wasn't ready, and I would let her know when, because to see you meant I had to face my past, which I was not prepared to do.*

*When I saw you at the Women's Clinic that day, I didn't recognize you at first, but the more I thought about it, I realized who you were. It was confirmed when I got home and pulled out the pictures your aunt had sent me of you.*

*I've looked back on that day and realized that I wasted an opportunity to get to know you, but the truth is, I was a coward. I was so embarrassed for you to see me there.*

*I want you to know that I was happy to find out that you were not there to have an abortion, but was there with a friend. It was a big relief. I don't want you to ever follow in my footsteps.*

*I'm so sorry for not being there for you, and I hope, one day, you find it in your heart to forgive me.*

*Sharon*

Mercedes cleared her throat. "Autumn, I'm so sorry sweetheart, I didn't know." She wiped her tears.

"I didn't either," I said, still shocked from the details of the letter. "How old are you?"

"I'm twenty."

"Wow."

"So how did you know Sharon had passed?"

"I'm in college here in Chicago. Like she said in the letter, she saw me at the clinic. I knew who she was, but I was so angry to see her there to get an abortion, my emotions got the best of me."

"How were you so sure it was Sharon?" Mercedes asked.

"Because I have parked outside this house many times, but could never get up the nerve to knock on the door. I've watched her come and go." She wiped a tear that managed to escape from her eye.

We talked for hours getting to know Autumn, and her getting to know us. We told her about the baby. Surprisingly, she didn't get angry.

She was very excited and even offered to babysit for us.

We talked about Sharon's final days, and what led up to her death. We tried to leave out the part about the affair, but she quickly called us on it. She told us she had followed Sharon one day, so she knew about the affair.

The time came for her to leave and get back to campus. I told her she was welcome anytime.

She and Mercedes planned to spend time together the following weekend. I think they have already begun to bond.

That night, I sat in my office, thinking about all the things that had happened in the last few months. So many of us affected in some way or another. Even from the grave, lies, betrayal, and deceit continue.

My heart ached for Autumn because she will never get to know her mother, and for the two babies, Sharon aborted that never got the chance to live their lives. And finally for me, because all I ever wanted was a family, a life full of laughter and adventure, for us to grow old together, but she took all of that away.

# Epilogue

"Hey man, you mind if I have a seat right here?"

"Nah, it's cool."

"Thanks. Let me buy you a beer."

"You don't have to do that."

"No problem. Bartender, let me get two coronas. I'm Tony, by the way."

"Richard."

"So, are you on vacation?"

"No, I live here."

"Aw, that's cool."

"What about you?"

"Oh, I'm on vacation. Tell you the truth, though. I wouldn't mind living here, the women are fine!"

"Hell yeah, that's why I'm here."

Both men laughed.

"Are you here with someone or just by yourself?"

"I'm here with a couple of my buddies."

"That's what's up."

"So, what do you locals do for fun here in good ole Costa Rica?"

"Man, there's so much to do here. It's all about what you like. I like to hang out down in the

Tamarindo. There are casinos, night clubs, and great food there."

"That sounds good."

"I can show you around if you like."

"Cool, I'll let them know."

"Well, if you guys want to get together tonight, I can take you to the hot spots."

"That would be great! Can I get your number?"

"Yeah, 555-5555?"

"What's yours?"

"555-1111?

"Hold on, let me answer this."

"Hello. Yes, at the bar. Okay, I'll be here. Sorry about that."

"No problem."

"Man, if you are not in a hurry, hang around and meet my buddies. They are on their way. They're coming from the room."

"You guys are staying in this hotel?"

"No, the one across the street."

"Okay."

"Bartender, give me two more coronas."

They continued to make small talk. Shortly after that, two police officers entered the bar.

"Richard, these are my buddies?"

"Whoa-what!" He said, as he did a double-take. He took a swallow of his beer, trying not to lose his cool.

"Richard Madison, I'm detective Millings with the Chicago Investigation Unit. You are under arrest for the attempted murder of Byron Jefferson."

The officer handcuffed Richard and took him into custody. "You, my friend, are going away for a very long time."

Richard hung his head down. He sat quietly in the back of the patrol car, preparing himself for the long road ahead.

www.ingramcontent.com/pod-product-compliance
Lightning Source LLC
Chambersburg PA
CBHW022144050726
47590CB00002B/573